The Wooden Rose

A symbol of love, a mystery unravelled…

By

Soraya

Blessings

Soraya

Also by Soraya

Book of Spells

Book of Tarot

Book of Runes

Enhance Your Psychic Powers

Reiki Training Manual

Soraya's Book of Psychic Answers

The Witches Companion

The Kitchen Witch

The Little Book of Spells

The Little Book of Cord and Candle Magick

To be published soon; The Practical Witch

Next in the Rose Trilogy, a prequel,

Before the Rose, The Gypsy's Curse

Copyright © 2015 Soraya

All rights reserved.

Copyright © 2015 Soraya

All rights reserved.

Table of Contents

Chapter 47

Acknowledgements

Coincidences:

Chapter 1

1889 A Travellers' Camp near Glasgow Green

"Hurry Rosa yer Da wants tae leave in ten minutes."

"Ah'm hurryin Ma, Ah'm goin' as fast as Ah can," said Rosa. She could hardly think straight as she hopped about pulling on her black boots and fastening the laces. She was excited at the thought of seeing Eddie again, tall handsome Eddie with his dark curly hair. She couldn't remember the first time that she saw him, but she had known all her life that he was hers. The last time they had met was at Musselburgh Fair when all the travellers got together to reunite, share good times, meet up with family and friends, and trade with each other.

She was sixteen now, her raven black hair came half way down her back and her green eyes shone under long dark eyelashes. Soon she would marry, and the only boy she would marry was Eddie. Her young heart fluttered when she thought of him. Eddie was so clever with his hands. He was an artist with wood, he didn't just make things, he made beautiful things. He made shelves for his Mam's precious ornaments, and he had carved the shapes himself and painted flowers and ivy down the sides. He made clothes pegs to sell round the doors too, but that was different.

Rosa carried a wooden token in her pocket. When no one was watching, she would take the token out of her pocket, look at it, and think of Eddie. Her Eddie had made it for her when he was fourteen and she was only ten. He had carved a lovely rose on the surface of it, and each time she looked at it or held it in her pocket, she thought of her Eddie. It was just a simple piece of wood, flat, about two inches across and half an inch thick, but she could feel the love in it. She was never without it and had never shown it to anyone. It was something special to her and Eddie.

"Hurry up lass," her father called as he hitched the horses to the front of the wagon.

"Stop yer day dreamin' and get up on the wagon."

She loved her Father; he was a big strong man with black curly hair, arms like tree trunks and hands like shovels. They were taking horses he had bred and trained to trade at the fair.

They were leaving Glasgow today, and it would be two or three days before they would reach Musselburgh. Soon they would meet up with friends and family. There would be horseracing and reunions. The young girls would be posing and showing off new dresses that their mothers or grannies had sewn for them, and young men, boys really, would be strutting and acting manly. Everything had to be perfect in this very proud culture and each family would vie to be and have the best; everyone went to Musselburgh Fair, it was traditional.

Mary's Mother had taught her how to scrub, clean, stack, and stow everything that they needed in, on, and around the big wagon. Pots and pans hung from the sides of the wagon and sang a merry note as they travelled. Everything was spic and span, for they were fussy about cleanliness.

Each night after a long day in the wagon, John would stop in the same place that his family had done for generations before him. There were trees to shelter the tent that they would put down to sleep in, because the wagon would be full of things that they needed when they were travelling and things that they could sell or swop. There was lush grass for the horses to graze on, and a running stream nearby for fresh water.

As soon as the wagon stopped, Mary and Rosa would jump down and begin to unpack the things they would need. They always carried wood to start the fire and Rosa would set that out. Mary would gather the slats from where they were stored under the wagon and she would use these to build a floor for their tent. They often erected their big tent if they were staying somewhere for a week or more, but when they were travelling, the smaller tent was fine for their needs.

With the fire started, Rosa helped her mother while John roped off an area and untied the trading horses from the wagon before turning them loose in the secured space. The lead horses were unhitched and turned loose with the others.

Their two terriers ran around excited to be free, but their big lurcher Suzie was tethered safely, with just enough rope to wander a short distance, otherwise she would have been off exploring and hunting for game. Mary set up the chitty prop, a three legged cast iron pyramid shape with a large hook for holding a pot over a fire, as Rosa fetched the water. Fire lit, kettle on to boil water for tea, and animals tended to, they could now sit and rest a while under the stars.

This is how they travelled; always following familiar routes and stopping at familiar places, each place would hold memories of previous times and previous journeys. Each morning they would rise early, feed the animals and stow all their belongings back in and around the wagon and continue on their journey.

As they neared Musselburgh, they would catch sight of others travelling to the fair and there was a stir of excitement in the air. Finally, they arrived and lined up in a queue to enter the grassy field. They waved and called to other families arriving or queuing. They could see the Morrison's, the Wilson's, and the Boswell's and there were others approaching that they would know, and some of their own family, their second cousins, the Stewarts, would be there too.

Rosa could hardly contain herself.

"Mind yer ane business Rosa and dinnae let yer Da catch you ey'in up these boys," her mother whispered.

Rosa was horrified and embarrassed "I'm no ey'in up boys, Ah was jist lookin' for…"

"I know who yer lookin for," replied her mother. "It's that Eddie McGuigan. A guid boy mind ye, but dinnae show yer keen."

Rosa blushed and her ears were burning with embarrassment.

"I like him Ma, he asked me to remember him last year."

"Wheesht, here's yer Da!"

Chapter 2

It was a hard life being a traveller, but it was a good life and a life that they loved. Mary, Rosa's mother, was a good-looking woman of average height and build, but it was her dark hair and eyes and her self-confidence that made her stand out. She always knew what to do and got on with doing it. There was nothing shy or retiring about Mary, and that was what her husband Johnny loved most about her.

Mary always got what she wanted, and in her younger days, she had had a nasty mean streak about her, but that was before she and John got together. She was more understanding and tolerant as an adult than she had ever been. He was known everywhere for his knowledge and skill with the horses, and it was probably that same skill that he used on Mary, settling her when she was about to fly off in a tantrum, or calming her when she was agitated.

Mary had two loves in her life; Rosa, her darling daughter and John, her big strong husband who in spite of his outward stern appearance, had a soft kindly heart and would do anything to help another. John didn't take any nonsense from anyone though, and could drive a hard bargain making sure that he got the best of any deal.

The sun was shining as John was unhitching his horses from the wagon while Mary and Rosa began to fetch the makings for their tent. They unloaded slats of wood from underneath the wagon for the big tent and with the help of nearby children; they began to put it together.

The wooden shapes for the floor went down first to establish the hexagon shape, leaving an uncovered space in the centre for the stove that they carried with them. Other children would dash in to help, and each would hold a length of wood while Mary and Rosa secured poles to the tops, holding the frame together and maintaining the shape.

There was lots of laughing and teasing as the children supported the frame, then Rosa and Mary, standing on either side of the frame began to throw and catch a big tarpaulin cover up and over. The tarpaulin had cords attached at various points to make the job of pulling the cover over easier.

Often they collapsed on the ground laughing and rubbing their aching arms from the effort of the task. Coloured cloths were fetched from the wagon and draped on the inside walls, and rugs were laid on the boards.

Finally, the stove was set up in the middle of the floor, and a long pipe attached to fit directly under the smoke hole at the top of the tent. The stove would keep them warm at night and with a kettle at the ready, there was always a cuppa for anyone who called in.

Outside, Mary set up the chitty prop, and young Rosa fetched the wood to start the fire. Before long, a large cast iron pot of soup or stew would be hanging from the chitty prop. Food was always cooked outside, keeping the tent free from smells and spills. There was always plenty to share among friends and family members.

The muscles in Eddie's arms bulged below the rolled up sleeves of his red and black checked shirt as he set up at the fair though he was oblivious to the admiring glances from some of the young girls. Thick dark hair framed his handsome face tanned with the summer sun. All he could think about was seeing his Rosa.

Eddie was a hard worker and talented too, he just put his head down and got on with things, and when he was working with wood, his mind would drift off into his plans for the future, the future he saw with Rosa. He knew that he was going to marry Rosa and that they would make a family together.

He could see it in his mind's eye as though it had already happened. A big family, boys and girls; the girls would help their Mam and marry well and the boys, well they would work with him. He would teach them how to look at a windfall tree trunk that others would pass by, and he would show them how to read the wood and see what things they could make from it. He would teach his sons how to create beautiful pieces of work that the wealthy would have on show in their fancy homes.

He was twenty now and had been learning to hone his gift for carpentry since he was a child, starting off just whittling bits of wood into little ornaments, making clothes pegs and selling them door to door. Eddie progressed to making three-legged stools and by the time he was in his teens, he was making special pieces; wooden spoons for stirring the pot, bowls, beautifully turned, carved and polished, containers with lids for sugar and tea, children's pull along toys, garden furniture, and wooden ornaments that the wealthy were happy to purchase. He had made good money and saved every penny he could. He was going to speak to Rosa's Father when he saw him next. He knew he could give her a good life with the money he had put by and his plans for the future.

Rosa was helping her mother to set up their camp when out of the corner of her eye she saw Eddie approaching. She glanced quickly at her mother as her cheeks began to glow bright red.

"Ma," she whispered.

"I see him."

Rosa kept her eyes downcast as Eddie approached, and not once did Eddie look in her direction.

"Excuse me, Aunty Mary," he said, as was the custom in his culture, "Could Ah speak tae Uncle John?"

"Ye've never had a problem speakin' tae him before Eddie, dae ye think ye might have wan the noo."

Eddie shuffled his feet showing his discomfort, but he could see that Mary was teasing him. Just at that moment, Uncle John appeared back from chatting to other family members who had just arrived.

"Eddie," he said, looking at Eddie sternly under heavy dark bushy eyebrows. Eddie's stomach might have been churning, but that was no comparison to what John was feeling. He knew in his soul what was coming, but he wasn't ready to let the apple of his eye, his little Rosa, go that easily.

"Uncle John, a word."

"Well, spit it out and Ah'm warnin' ye, Ah'm nae in the best o moods,"

Eddie bristled at John's sharp tone. "Ah could come back an' see ye."

"Jist git on wi' it lad, Ah've things tae dae."

Eddie drew himself up to his full height, stuck out his chin and his chest, looked his uncle in the eye, and said, "It's an important thing Ah wish tae speak tae ye about, but if ye huvnae time tae be civil Ah'll come back."

"Jist haud yer horses' lad, ye got me on the wrong foot. Ah feel Ah know whit ye want to speak tae me about an it's churnin' in ma' stomach. Say yer piece."

John stepped closer to Eddie to put his arm over his shoulder. Surprised by the fact that Eddie was taller than he thought, he wondered why he hadn't noticed, he was dealing with a full-grown man now, but in his mind and heart, to John, Eddie was still a lad. He did what any other proud man would do to avoid his embarrassment, and stuck his hands in his pockets.

"Let's take a walk," he said to the young man.

They walked in silence away from the hustle and bustle of everyone chatting and setting up for the fair. Both men were a generation apart, but both with the same person in mind. Finally, Eddie stopped, looked his uncle in the eye as he looked back at him, took a deep breath, and said, "Ah've loved yer lass since Ah was wee, an' she was just a babe. Ah've watched her grow and become the beautiful lass like the flower ye named her for. The past four years Ah've worked and saved and every penny is for Rosa's future."

His uncle fixed his gaze on him, just stared at him silently saying nothing while his mind went into overdrive.

The words poured out of Eddie like a desperate plea. "Ah'm askin' ye for her hand man," he almost shouted.

John stared at him, the fear becoming a reality, the pain of that reality written on his face.

"Same time, same place, next year, if ye still feel the same ye can ask her yirsel, an' if she agrees ye can marry on the first day of May at the Tinkers Heart."

Eddie's face lit up, he punched the air and did a dance right there in front of John.

"She'll say aye, I know it."

Eddie ran off back to his pitch and as John walked back to his wagon he watched Rosa helping her mother.

"Ah've jist seen that young Eddie," he said to no one in particular, but really so that Rosa could hear. "Turned into a fine man," he said, and climbed into his wagon where he poured himself a whisky, sat down and stared at the wall in front of him, seeing nothing but the memories of his daughter's birth and early years. Thinking of her blossoming into a beautiful woman, he wondered how he would feel to let her go, to start her own life. When Mary came in his face was wet with tears, she sat beside him and reached over, placed her hand in his and gave it a comforting squeeze. No words were necessary between them for she understood how he felt.

Chapter 3

The atmosphere at the Musselburgh Fair was electric and exciting. Friends and families merged and mingled, lurchers and terriers barked, children played, and the men did what men do. They traded horses, ponies, and dogs, showed their Persian rugs, tin pots and other crafts and looked on proudly at their sons and daughters. They exchanged wares and ideas on how to make a living, places to go to sell their wares, and places to avoid.

The men were a sight to see, all wearing jackets, flat caps, and often waistcoats below. Shirts tucked into dark trousers were clean and white with no collars, but a colourful patterned scarf at the neck. They all stood in a group making loud exchanges as they performed the almost religious ceremony of trading and bargaining. With each offer or counter offer, the men would slap hands, but even that had a specific format. A spit on the palm and a full-handed slap was a deal, but if only fingertips slapped then the bargaining would continue. The seller held his hand out asking, and the buyer would state his offer and slap. The men had idiosyncrasies that would give each other clues to what they were thinking. Some would touch their caps between slaps. Some would turn and pretend to be walking away. Others would complain loudly and throw accusations, but there was always a bargain sealed.

A horse buyer would gradually make his way around so that he could stand directly in front of the horse seller and pretend to be mildly interested. He might stroke the horse, have a look at its teeth, pick up a leg, and feel its joints. The seller would know by this that a sale was imminent and the bargaining would begin.

"Guid enough horse." (Slap)

"What'll ye offer?" (Slap)

"Forty an' not a penny more." (Slap)

"Ah yer jokin' man; Sixty an' not a penny less." (Slap)

"Sixty? Yer a robber Ah'll give forty-five." (Slap)

"Fifty an' ye have a deal."

A spit on the palm and a hand held out, a spit on the palm and a full-handed slap and the deal done.

"Now gimmie a penny back for luck," the buyer would say, and as was the custom, the seller would give the buyer a coin or two and the bargain was sealed.

Young men would stand by and watch the exchanges learning the craft, and then they would discuss among themselves the skills or failings that they had witnessed.

"Aye, he couldha got cheaper," or "He couldha got more if he hung oot a bit."

They in their way would take on board lessons that they had learned, that they would use themselves when their time came. Overloaded with testosterone, they rode their horses bareback, raced each other, and performed tricks to impress the girls. The girls giggled and looked coy and pretended to be unimpressed by the boys.

In the middle of all this, the women gossiped and bragged about their children while they skinned hares for the pot. Some chopped vegetables and fetched split peas and lentils that had been soaked overnight. Dumplings and potatoes added to the stew ensured that there was plenty of filling food all.

Everyone gathered around the campfires and shared the food that had been prepared earlier in the day, and then out would come the pipes and the tobacco for a relaxing smoke. Some of the old grannies would smoke a clay pipe and ponder while they remembered and shared stories about their own younger days.

Those that could play a tune would fetch a musical instrument, fiddles would be fine-tuned, flutes prepared, and box accordions stretched and squeezed. Some would have the traditional Celtic drum the bodhran, and others would be happy with a tambourine or a set of spoons. Others still, with no instrument, would sit open legged on a wooden box and tap a rhythm on the box to accompany the music.

The women and girls would dance and twirl on boards laid out for the purpose; boxes were set out around the space for others to sit on and participate, playing an instrument, or singing, or just enjoying the spectacle. The atmosphere was warm, friendly and exciting, the smell of wood smoke from the fire scented the air, and the night was clear and bright under the full of the moon.

Eddie and Rosa sat side by side quietly chatting. She felt pretty in her new dress, with its full drindle skirt that she had helped her mother to sew. With her head down, she studied the bright blues and reds of the fabric as she wondered what to say to Eddie. They both felt different now that Eddie had declared his intentions. He told Rosa what her father had said. For now, they could sit together or hold hands, perhaps even sneak a kiss if no one was watching, but all eyes would be on them now for it's the traveller's way to be chaste before marriage.

After the fair, the only way that they could communicate would be by messages passed by word of mouth, or for those that could read and write, and at that time, there were only a few with this skill, a note. It would be twenty years before a public telephone appeared, but there were so many of their kind that it was always possible to pass a message from one to another by those who were moving from place to place.

"Ah'm sixteen now, next August when we come to the fair next year Ah'll be seventeen. If ma Da says we can marry on the first of May Ah'll be nearly eighteen an' you'll be nearly twenty-two. It all seems so far away," she said as she looked into his dark brown eyes. His dark curly hair fell over his brow and curled over his collar at the back. They were so entranced with each other that at first they were unaware of the chant.

"Rosa, Rosa, Rosa, give us a dance."

She giggled and got up and moved to the centre of the circle and gave an exaggerated bow. Everyone knew Rosa loved to dance, and had she not been so engrossed in conversation with Eddie, she would have been the first to start the dancing.

The fiddle stuck up, the flutes joined, and the circle of folk began to clap in time to the music. The bodhran beat out its rhythm and Rosa threw her head back with a laugh. She began to dance a jig, her feet matching the rhythm on the boards. She held her skirts up a tiny bit and her black laced boots were visible below them. Round and round the circle she danced, skipping and twirling, the sound of her heels joining the beat of the music, her dark hair flying behind her and then she began to pull other girls into the circle where they joined in the fun of the dance. She was so happy that she wished she was married to Eddie now, and that this could be the beginning of their life together.

As the night ended, a singing voice filled the air and Rosa knew that it was her Father. He was singing the song that his Father used to sing to his Mother.

Johnny was born in a mansion doon in the county o' Clare

Rosie was born by a roadside somewhere in County Kildare

Destiny brought them together on the road to Killorglan

One day in her bright tasty shawl, she was singing

And she stole his young heart away

For she sang...

Meet me tonight by the campfire

Come with me over the hill.

Let us be married tomorrow

Please let me whisper 'I will'

What if the neighbours are talkin'

Who cares if yer friends stop and stare

Ye'll be proud to be married to Rosie,

Who was reared on the roads of Kildare.

Think of the parents who reared ye

Think of the family name

How can ye marry a gypsy?

Oh whit a terrible shame

Parents and friends stop yer pleading

Don't worry aboot my affair

For Ah've fallen in love wi' a gypsy

Who was reared on the roads of Kildare?

Johnny went down from his mansion

Just as the sun had gone doon

Turning his back on his kinfolk

Likewise, his dear native toon

Facing the roads of old Ireland

Wi' a gypsy he loved so sincere

When he came to the light of the campfire

These are the words he did hear

Meet me tonight by the campfire

Come wi' me over the hill.

Let us be married tomorrow

Please let me whisper 'I will'

What if the neighbours are talkin?

Who cares if yer friends stop and stare

Ye'll be proud to be married to Rosie,

Who was reared on the roads of Kildare.

Chapter 4

Travelling families rarely built their own wagons, but Eddie's skills with wood enabled him to do just that, and he wanted Rosa to have the best that he could make. A farmer on the outskirts of Glasgow sold him a small piece of land; Eddie fenced it and built a shed. Whenever he passed a wood yard or sawmill on his travels, he would call in to see what they had. From time to time, he purchased timbers to lay aside so that he could build a wagon for Rosa that he would present to her on their wedding day.

Most of the wagons that he was familiar with had a narrow floors and sides that sloped outwards, but he had seen some showmen at one of the fairs. Their wagons had a wider floor, were taller with a slightly pitched roof, and windows on both sides. He was going to build that style of wagon for himself and Rosa to begin their new life. He had been gathering oak, ash, walnut, and pine and he would use all of it to make the finest wagon that anyone had ever seen. In his mind's eye, he could see the travelling home he would build. It might take a year or more, but he would work night and day if he had to.

Eddie shared his parent's wagon, and he was proud of the work that he had done on it, taking it from a standard style to something that turned heads wherever they went. Their wagon had a narrow floor encased between tall wheels making it safer for travelling over streams and rough ground.

The original body of the wagon had curved support struts covered in a thick canvas. Eddie had remodelled the original interior making cabinets for storage from the floor to waist height. In the centre of the cabinets, he fitted a small pot-bellied stove with a chimney flue running up to the top emerging from one side to allow smoke from the stove to escape.

Eddie fashioned the canvas cover, cutting it into sections that overlapped for protection from the weather and on fine days, sections could be tied back to let in light and air. At the front and back, he added porches with carved side brackets and then painted fancy scroll patterns along the brackets. He cut the door in two halves, allowing the top half of the door to be open while the bottom remained closed, and the addition of strong ropes to the steps allowed the family to raise or lower them at will. Pots, pans, and other necessities hung from racks he fitted along the outsides. The intricately carved wood was brightly painted and polished until it shone like glass. Gold leaf added the final additions to his work of art.

Eddie's parents, Edward and Nellie, were very proud of their only child. Eddie travelled with his parents, but he had his own horse and cart that he used to carry his wares. He spent his days going from door to door selling what he had and when they weren't travelling to fairs he would ride over to his shed and work until late, building the wagon for his Rosa.

Eddie and Rosa managed to see each other now and then when they were attending the same fairs, but Rosa was sad every time they had to part. By the following August when they returned to Musselburgh Fair Eddie had finished building the wagon, and he would spend the next months after the fair painting and decorating the outside, so that it would be completed in time for their wedding in May.

Rosa was watching for him coming, her stomach churning with eager anticipation. She caught sight of him as he jumped down from his cart and they ran to each other. He picked her up in his arms and swung her around in a circle before setting her down and looking into her eyes.

"Aye lass, yer as beautiful as I remember, have ye missed me?"

"Oh Eddie, Ah thought of ye every day."

The thought of parting even for a moment was unbearable for both of them.

Later that day, when everyone had seen to their horses and set up their tents, Eddie took Rosa for a walk along the River Esk. They sat on a log by a tree on the banks of the river, and Eddie took Rosa's hands in his and looked into her eyes.

"On the first of May next year we'll marry above Loch Fyne at the Tinkers Heart, and Ah promise Ah'll love ye forever Rosa if ye'll have me."

He reached into his pocket, took out a beautiful gold ring with tiny diamonds in the shape of a flower, and placed the ring on her finger.

"Aye Eddie, Ah will marry ye," Rosa said, and he kissed the happy tears on her face.

The festive air was richer that night by the announcement that Rosa Stewart was to marry Eddie McGuigan, and people came up to offer their best wishes to the happy couple. Many promised that they would make the long journey to The Tinkers Heart at Loch Fyne to share and witness the marriage between the two families. When the fair was over the loving couple had to part and go their separate ways, and it was likely that the next time that they would see each other would be at the Tinkers Heart on their wedding day

Rosa spent the following months gathering and making things for her bottom drawer. Every girl had to have a bottom drawer, more often it was a trunk, and she would keep things in it for her own travelling home when she married.

She would often open it and look through her things, handling them with love and care and thinking of what it would be like to be Eddie's wife. Inside her trunk were white linen pillowcases and sheets, hand laced by pulling the ten weft threads an inch below the hems, and then gathering the warp threads together using embroidery silks creating patterns of little crosses around each edge.

She knew how to do that too now that her Mother had taught her. Another set of linen trimmed with lace lay in the trunk, and she knew that when she married there would be more gifts from travelling families everywhere. There was a lovely china tea set handed down to use for very special occasions, and some small ornaments that she had collected over the years.

Pride of place among her things was a box that Eddie had made and given to her when they parted on the last day of the Musselburgh Fair. It was about eight inches long, four inches wide, and four inches deep. Eddie had carved the top of the box with fancy scrollwork, and anyone seeing it would recognise Eddie's work immediately. It was a beautiful keepsake and looking at it reminded Rosa how much they loved each other.

As Rosa thought of Eddie, his mind would drift to her while he concentrated on painting the new wagon. Inside he had built storage cupboards in every conceivable space.

His cousin Tam had given him a hand to position the cast iron stove that he built against a wall, which he had faced with tiles to prevent the wood from overheating. The flue ran up the wall and out at the top of the side and a tiled slab beneath the stove protected the floor. The top of the stove had a flat surface so that Rosa could boil a pot of soup or a kettle for tea on the colder days, for in the summer time a campfire outside and the chitty pot was preferred.

Eddie had thought everything through before he started his build and he was not disappointed with the result. It was just one large room, but Eddie had created pull out panels so that the room would divide into sections. There was plenty of room for two comfortable chairs and a table. He could see himself and Rosa sitting there enjoying a chat or a cuppa after a days' work.

He carved and painted the facings on the shelves and cupboards with several coats of paint, and the outside of the wagon was similarly carved, decorated, and finished with gold leaf. Boxes and racks fitted to the sides meant they could carry or store their wares, their cooking utensils, and anything else that they would need while they were on the road.

Eddie had cleverly created an overhang at the front of the wagon so that whoever was leading the horses wouldn't get wet on rainy days, and another at the back so that anyone sitting at the back would benefit from the shelter. He would hitch a trailer behind the wagon filled with the tools of his trade, horse feed, and their tent.

He was very proud of his achievement, and planned to present it to Rosa during the festivities after the wedding ceremony. He tried to picture her reaction to seeing it for the first time. On the journey to Loch Fyne, the new wagon would be concealed under a heavy tarpaulin so that Rosa would be the first to see it.

Chapter 5

Four weeks before the wedding Mary brought out a box and opened it to reveal the dress that she had worn on her wedding day. The fine cotton lawn fabric was a very pale blue colour, with tiny sprigs of white daisies all over it. The scooped neckline had a delicate blue ribbon drawstring, finished with a trim of hand-made lace and this matched the cuffs of the long sleeves. Rosa tried it on and looked down at herself. The hem of the dress came to just above her ankles and over the dress was a white lace pinafore, which came to a point at the front just above the hem.

Smiling and with tears in her eyes Mary unwrapped a brown paper parcel, to reveal a long net veil which was trimmed from top to bottom in the same lace which matched the dress. A circlet of tiny handmade flowers held the veil in place. Mary held a looking glass in front of Rosa and she gazed at her reflection.

"Oh Ma, Ah look, Ah look beautiful." She said this as though she had no idea how lovely she was.

"Ye are that Rosa, yer the most bonny bride Ah have ever seen. Quick now tak it aff afore yer Da comes back, and Ah'll get it a' ready for yur big day."

There was no need for wedding invitations in the travelling community; by now, everyone would know that they were to be married at the Tinkers Heart, and as was the custom, hundreds of travellers began to make the journey during the last week in April. Some would make their way over the 'Rest and be Thankful' turning into Gleann Mor and over Hells Glen to reach the Tinkers Heart, and those that came from the direction of Inveraray would come by Cairndow and the shores of Loch Fyne.

When the camp was set up everyone prepared for the feasting and celebration. They had all brought gifts for Rosa and Eddie; some brought linen, rugs, pots and pans or dishes, others would give the couple an envelope filled with cash to give them a good start in life.

On the first morning of May, Eddie leading the way, they all climbed to the top of the hill, and up to the Tinkers Heart, which had quartz crystals laid out on the ground to form the heart shape. There was an air of celebration and laughter and some sang as they climbed.

There were herrin' heeds an' bits o' breed,

Herrin' heeds an' haddies O,

Herrin' heeds an' bits o' breed,

To carry on the weddin O

Voices rang out the chorus line

Drum-mer a-doo a-doo a-day,

Drum-mer a-doo a dad-din O

Drum-mer a-doo a-doo a-day,

Hurrah for the Tinker's weddin O

It was a fine day, the sun was shining as Rosa and her Father followed the party climbing through the gorse and the heather. The scent of bog myrtle filled the air as their clothes brushed past the wild shrubs. John held Rosa's hand in his firm grip as they climbed the hill. Lizzie, Rosa's cousin and bridesmaid, walked behind holding up Rosa's delicate veil to protect it from the wild gorse or brambles that grew on the hillside.

"Ah'm so proud oh ye lass, ye look mer beautiful the day than a have ever seen ye. Ah cannae tell ye how much yer Ma an me are gonnae miss ye lass, but Eddie's a guid lad an it's aye been you an' him. He'll look after ye of that Ah'm sure."

"Ah know Da, Ah know, Ah'll miss you an' Ma tae. Ah've aye known we'd be wed Da"

From the top of the hill, they looked across at the opposite shore where they could see Dunderave Castle and over to the west lay Inveraray. Cairndow was at the bottom of the hill where the vicar had come from to perform the ceremony.

As they walked between fellow travellers, friends and families Rosa caught sight of Eddie for the first time and her heart skipped a beat. So handsome he was standing there, his piercing brown eyes filled with love as he stared at her. He looked fine in a new brown suit, and his dark hair curled over the collar of his white shirt. Her Father led her towards Eddie who was standing at the quartz heart, he placed her hand in Eddie's, and with a lump in his throat and a tear in his eye, he stepped back to join Mary. Tam, Eddie's cousin, stood by his side performing the duty of best man, and he carried the gold ring that Eddie would place on her finger never to be taken off.

After the ceremony, they all gathered back at the camp in the field by the loch and the celebrations began. There was feasting on jugged hare stew, roasted suckling pig, fresh caught wild salmon, and brown trout. After the feasting, out came the flutes, fiddles and squeezeboxes and the dancing and singing began in earnest.

I ken ye dinnae like it lass, the winter here in toon

For the scaldies a miscaw us, and they try tae bring us doon

And it's hard tae raise three bairns, in a single flae box room

But all tak ye on the road again, when the yella's on the broom

When the yella's on the broom, when the yella's on the broom

I'll tak ye on the road again, when the yella's on the broom

The scaldies ca us tinker dirt, and they spurn oor bairn's in school

But fa cares fit the scaldies think, for the scaldies, but a fool

They never hear the yarlin's song, nor see the flaxen bloom

For they're cooped up in hooses when the yella's on the bloom

Nae sale for pegs or baskets noo that used to bide our lives

But I seem to work at scaldies jobs, from nine o' clock till five

But we ca' nae man oor maister, when we own the warld roon

And I'll bid fareweel tae Breechin, when the yella's on the broom

I'm weary for the springtime, when we tak the road aince mair

Tae the plantin and the fermin, and the berry fields O Blair

When we meet up wi' oor kin-folk, frae a' the country roon

And we yarn aboot wha'll tak the road when the yella's on the broom

Unbeknown to Rosa, as planned, Eddie's cousin Tam had driven the new wagon, concealed under a tarpaulin, all the way to Loch Fyne. Eddie asked Rosa to wait where she was as he had something to do. Rosa was puzzled, but she agreed and sat with her family and friends while Eddie went off to fetch the wagon.

A short while later, when she heard the commotion, she turned and there was Eddie driving the covered wagon led by two fine horses. He jumped down from the wagon and as everyone watched, Tam and Eddie drew back the tarpaulin amid admiring gasps and cheers from the partygoers.

"This is for ye ma darling, a weddin present tae start oor life the gether, this is yer new home."

She thought it was the biggest wagon she had ever seen, and the wooden trims were intricately carved, and painted in bright colours. A proud Eddie helped Rosa up onto the wagon while everybody was cheering, banging posts and shouting good wishes to the happy couple. There were murmurs of appreciation as everyone crowded around to admire Eddie's handiwork and later several of the guests spoke to Eddie, asking if he could build similar wagons for them. Eddie could see that this would be a good way to make a living; doing something, he loved doing with Rosa by his side. Much later, Eddie and Rosa, proudly seated at the front of the wagon, left the wedding amid cheers, well wishes, and laughter, to camp further down the on the loch side.

Mary and John had given Eddie Rosa's trunk, and he had set it to one side in the wagon for her to find. When they arrived at the loch side, while Eddie unhitched the horses and set out food and water for them, Rosa went into the wagon.

The first thing she saw was her precious trunk. She knelt on the floor and opened it. Looking at her things made her think of her Mother and her Father, and although she was blissfully happy, she was also a little sad knowing that she was leaving her childhood behind and becoming a wife.

Chapter 6

By the time Eddie came back in from seeing to the horses, Rosa had set a small fire in the stove with the kettle on the hot plate. There was a slight chill to the night air, but the wagon was nice and warm.

"Would ye like some tea Eddie?"

"Aye lass that Ah would."

Both Rosa and Eddie were nervous, but the simple act of having a cup of tea settled them. For a short while, they chatted about how much everyone had enjoyed and participated in the wedding and their lovely gifts.

Before too long, Rosa was in Eddies embrace, he was gentle and caring as he drew her into his arms and kissed her tenderly. Such was their passion that night that his seed took hold and within a few weeks, Rosa began to notice the changes in her body. She knew immediately that a new life was growing inside her. Eddie was overjoyed when she told him, and he picked her up, swung her around, and kissed her face over and over again.

"Oh ma love, ma lass. Ye have made me the happiest man alive."

Soon they were into their own routine travelling from place to place, where Eddie sold his woodcraft and took orders from customers, and Rosa spent her time organising and cleaning her new home and cooking a meal for Eddies return. There was always time to spare, and Rosa used that time to make small posies of dried flowers and lace doilies to sell round doors in villages they came across.

They planned to spend their first year travelling from place to place, setting up camp, selling their wares, and meeting friends and families far afield that had not been able to travel to their wedding. They would return to camp near Glasgow Green at the end of October, so that they could be close to Mary and John before the baby was due.

Rosa did not have an easy time in her pregnancy; in the beginning it was just morning sickness, and usually Eddie was gone before it took hold of her, but as the weeks passed she wondered how other woman coped as those that she knew seemed to take it in their stride

By the time Rosa was five months pregnant, she was plagued with headaches, and sometimes, dizzy spells overwhelmed her, and she would have to lie down until the feeling passed. Her face, hands, feet, and legs were very swollen and she was always tired. Eddie was worried about her and did his best to look after her, but she never admitted to him how badly she felt.

This was her first child and she did not realise that these things were not normal. She stoically carried on with her daily chores of cleaning and cooking, but as each day passed she found it harder and harder to get out of bed. She was embarrassed and didn't want to admit that she wasn't coping. She was afraid that others would think she was just complaining for the sake of it.

"Women have babies all the time," she thought.

When they arrived back at the camp in Glasgow at the end of October she was seven months pregnant. Mary took one look at her and cried in dismay.

"Oh my God Rosa, look at you. Yer so swollen, that's no normal. Quick John, get Eddie get this wean tae the hospital."

Eddie came running in. "Whit's wrang?"

"She's sick son, Ah think she's got the toxins. We need to get her tae the hospital at Castle Street."

Eddie and John hitched a small cart and made it ready to carry Rosa and Mary to the hospital, but by the time they reached it Rosa was as white as a sheet, and barely conscious.

"Whit's wrong wi' her Ma, will she be awright?" Eddie asked.

"Rosa darlin, speak to me, why did ye no tell me ye wernae well."

She reached out and held his hand as tears ran down her face.

"Save ma baby!" she said, "Save ma baby an' call her Rosie."

"No Rosa, no, wur nearly there yer gonnae be awright."

Tears ran down Eddie's face as he held Rosa in his arms. John ran into the hospital and came back seconds later with nurses and a trolley. They helped to lift Rosa on to the trolley and whisked her away from them. Mary, John, and Eddie, followed the trolley as far as the labour ward, and sat in the cold corridor clutching hands and crying together, praying that Rosa and the baby would be all right. Doctors and nurses hurried in and out of the door that they had taken Rosa through, and all they could do was sit and pray in silence. A nurse took them into a side room and brought them hot sweet tea.

An hour passed before they heard the faintest whimper, the first cry of baby Rosie. They rushed into the corridor with a sigh of relief until they saw the doctor coming towards them, his green scrubs covered in blood and a grim expression on his face. This was not the face of someone bearing good news. Something was wrong. He started the conversation with,

"I am very, very, sorry."

At that, two grown men fell to their knees.

Mary screamed at the top of her voice "Nooooo" she screamed "Nooooo," and she fell to the floor at the doctor's feet in a dead faint.

Little did they know that later, they would all feel that pain again…
much, much, later…

Baby Rosie was very premature, and at first, they did not think that she would survive, but she rallied quickly and the doctors agreed to release her to the care of her granny. Night and day, hardly sleeping, she sat with her, caring for her and loving her, pouring the same love that she had had for Rosa into the tiny baby. Friends and neighbours from the community gathered, as is their way, to look after things while Mary cared for her grandchild.

The dreadful day arrived when Rosa was to be put into the ground. The family gathered, with Eddie leading the procession with his cousin Tam supporting him as he carried his tiny baby in his arms. Mary and John with Eddie's parents came next, and all the members of their immediate community followed in two's, three's, and fours.

Along the way, travellers joined them, word of mouth having told them of the tragedy. Hundreds followed the sombre group as they made their way on this sad journey. A specially constructed cart, drawn by four white horses, carried Rosa's flower covered coffin to Janefield Cemetery in the Gallowgate.

Hundreds of travellers all wearing black, their heads bowed in sorrow were already gathered to meet the procession that walked behind the hearse. The Glasgow streets were crowded with people who lived nearby, and they stood along the pavements watching and whispering quietly.

Rosa's casket was lowered into the ground, and the mourners filed past dropping tokens into the grave onto Rosa's casket. Some dropped ivy leaves, others a piece of lace made into a flower shape. Others dropped small posies or a handful of soil.

At the end of the ceremony, Rosa's grave was completely dressed in wreaths and flower garlands, and the mourners stood in silence remembering beautiful Rosa, dancing at the Musselburgh Fairs and on her wedding day at the Tinkers Heart.

Sadder still was the sight of Eddie holding the tiny baby, wrapped warmly in a white hand crocheted woollen shawl, and wearing a warm hat and mittens. He looked a broken man, tears coursing down his face, supported as he was by John, Mary, and his own parents.

"It was the toxins that got her," people were saying.

Some would later know it as pre-eclampsia.

"She might have lived had she known it wisnae normal."

"Aye it's too late noo."

"When its yer time its yer time."

"Look at that poor lad, it's a shame, it saddens yer heart it does."

"How will he manage that bairn?"

"Mary will mind the bairn; Eddie's Ma's no fit. Mary an' John will see them awright."

"Eddies a canny lad, he's got a bit put by."

Eddie had asked Mary and John if they would move into his wagon to help care for baby Rosie. Since his wagon was big enough for the four of them, and they were spending most of their time there anyway, the decision was an easy one. Mary and John traded their wagon to another family, and from then on they all travelled together.

Chapter 7

Time passes as time does, and day by day the pain that Eddie and the family felt began to become bearable. Eddie worked hard giving all his time to building wagons for those that could afford his prices. The money he made was for Rosie's future, but he seldom said a word to anyone, least of all his daughter, but he looked at her. He watched her as she grew and played with other children; every time he looked at her, he could see Rosa in her and the pain was hard to bear. He found himself choked with grief any time he tried to talk to her. It was easier to walk away.

Granny Mary and Pa John on the other hand lavished the child with love and attention. She was often with one or the other and anything she wanted she got, though she seldom asked for anything other than to be around them all the time chatting and fussing and asking questions. She seldom went near her Father, her young mind sensing something and assuming that he had no time for her.

Eddie often spoke with his Rosa in his heart and sometimes he was sure he could hear her voice. She would talk to him about the child and chide him for his tears.

"Let me go Eddie," he would hear her say.

"Mind the bairn Eddie."

"Find another wife Eddie."

"Never," he would say aloud and end his secret conversation.

In 1914, when war was declared, Eddie was among the first of his family and community to volunteer. This was a sad and worrying time for everyone, not just for the travelling community. Those within the community that were too old or unfit took their women and children further into the country for safety's sake.

Many of the travelling women joined the land girls working on farms, ploughing fields using horse drawn ploughs, tending to animals, getting up at five in the morning for milking, and mucking out cowsheds.

Those travelling men that did return came back changed men forever. Some of these lads received medals for their services to King and country, but all of them had scars that would never heal, some in mind and some in body. It was a frightening time for everyone.

Mary was heartbroken that her John never made it home, but Eddie came back wounded in the leg, he was alive and home and that was the main thing. He never spoke of the things he had seen, or the friends and family members that had been lost, but he carried the sadness on his face as most folk did.

Tam came back; he had been one of the lucky ones, if anyone could be considered lucky. During a battle, his officer's horse panicked and threw the officer to the ground almost trampling him. Tam jumped forward, grabbed the frightened horse, and calmed it. He then assisted his officer to his feet and made sure that he was uninjured.

The officer was shaken, but unhurt, and he asked Tam where he got his horse skills. Tam explained his background and experience breeding and training horses, and within weeks, he was shipped back to England to train horses for the war effort. His time overseas had affected him badly though, and working with the horses he loved helped him to recover from the trauma he had experienced.

When the war was over and it was safe to go back to their normal camp by Gretna Green, so many things had changed. Builders were building new homes, and engineers were planning new roads to accommodate the cars that were now becoming more common. The old was beginning to merge with the new, and soon enough everyone began to settle into this new lifestyle.

Some travellers wanted to settle in houses when they returned, but most still loved the life of freedom and fresh air, living on and from the land. Eddie picked up his business where he left off, and once more those that could would go from door to door, selling their wares, sharpening knives, and odd jobbing wherever they could.

One day, when Rosie was about fourteen, she asked her Granny about a box that was on one of the high shelves. She had noticed it before, but had never thought to ask about it.

"Whit's in that box Granny?"

There was a silence.

"Granny, whit's in that box?"

Mary knew the day would come and here it was.

"It's some things belongin' tae yer mother."

"Whit things, are they mine, can Ah see? Please Granny let me see the box."

Mary reached up and handed the box to Rosie, who took it reverently, placed it on the table, and sat down staring at it. She stroked her hands across the top of the box, and then she looked up at her granny.

"Did ma Da make it?"

"Aye, he did."

"Did he make it for ma Ma?"

"Aye."

She stroked the wooden box again, passing her hands over the delicately carved roses and the etched pattern that ran all around the outside edges.

"Whit's in it Granny?"

"Precious things hinny."

"Can Ah open it?"

"Aye."

Rosie slowly opened it. Inside was a piece of lace from Rosa's wedding dress, all that was left of it, for she had been dressed in it for her burial. Her wedding ring had remained on her finger, but her engagement ring was in the box, along with a small circle of wood with a rose carved in the centre. Rosie picked up the ring and tried it on each of her fingers.

"One day when Ah'm bigger this might fit me; Ah'll be able tae wear it."

Mary glanced at her fondly.

"Aye ye will."

She put the ring back in the box and picked up the wooden carving. She pensively stroked a finger over the rose.

"He's clever ma Da tae make this."

"He made it when he was just a lad, and gave it tae yer Ma when she was jist a lass. She carried it awe the time an' thought nae body knew she had it but yer Pa an' me, we knew."

Rosie held it tightly in her hand and thought about the mother that she had never known. She loved her Granny, but she missed her Ma with a soreness that she couldn't put into words.

"Was she pretty Granny?"

"She was right bonnie an' she could sing an' dance better than the rest."

"Dae Ah look like her Granny?"

Mary's eyes were full of tears when she answered.

"Aye lass, yer her double. See for yir self there's a wee picture there."

Rosie picked up the small square photograph and there was her Father, younger and happier than she had ever seen him looking down at her Mother.

"She's beautiful granny."

She studied the images before her and thought of the mother she had never known. The sadness and emptiness inside her made her quiet for a while with her thoughts. She put the picture back in the box and picked up the wooden rose once more. She looked at her granny.

"Can a have it Granny?"

"I don't know lass ye'll have tae ask yer Da."

"He's outside. Will Ah ask him the noo?"

Mary looked outside to see Eddie feeding the horses.

"Go on then if ye like."

Rosie ran outside, "Da! Da! Can Ah speak tae ye?"

Eddie turned and looked down at her as she held up the carved wooden rose. She watched the colour drain from his face and then watched it come back until he was bright red with anger.

"Where did ye git that? Never mind!" he said, and stormed off away from the camp.

Rosie felt the tears welling in her throat. The pain in her heart was unbearable. She thought her father hated her so much that he couldn't bear to talk to her, but she needed him. She needed to talk to him, and she was going to, if he liked it or not. She gathered her courage and followed the path that her father had taken and caught sight of him sitting on a log by a stream. She approached softly and stood just behind him.

"Ah'm sorry a killed ma Ma. Ah'm sorry that ye hate me Da, an' Ah'm sorry that ye canny love me."

He turned sharply, and she was shocked to see tears coursing down his face. He stood and placed his hands on her shoulders and looking into her eyes he said, "Whit dae ye mean, ye killed yer Ma. Ye never killed yer Ma."

"But she died havin me," Rosie was crying too.

"No lass," he said, as he drew her towards him and held her in his arms for the first time since she was a baby.

"Yer Ma was dyin when we got to the hospital, an' there was nuthin wi' could dae, but the last thing she said tae me was 'Save ma baby, call her Rosie', she wanted you tae live."

He choked on his words; swallowing his tears, he said,

"An' Rosie Ah dae love ye, Ah love ye wi' aw' ma heart, it's jist every time Ah see ye Ah blame ma self for no understandin that yer Ma was awffy sick. If Ah had known maybe she couldha been saved."

They held each other tight, both cried cathartic tears, and then they talked as they had never talked before.

Rosie knew that she loved her father, but knowing that he loved her and that her mother's death wasn't her fault filled her with a new deeper love for her him and a happiness that she could not put into words. She looked at his handsome tanned face lined with worry as he spoke to her and for the first time he told her stories about himself and her mother.

He told her about the little wooden rose, remembering when he had carved it and remembering the day that he had given it to her.

"Ah'm glad yer Granny kept some stuff for ye, an" Ah'm heart sorry that Ah could nae tell ye aboot hur afore the noo."

Together they looked at the token that Rosie held in her hand.

"Can Ah carry it in ma pocket Da. Ah'll be careful wi it Ah promise?"

"Aye, of course ye can, yer Ma wid be happy aboot that."

As they walked back towards the wagon, Mary looked out of her window and cried "Oh!" as the tears poured from her eyes. There was Eddie, hand in hand with Rosie, she looking up at him and him looking down at her, and both of them happy and smiling at each other.

"Well Ah never, an' not afore time," Mary thought.

She moved away from the window and sitting at the table, opened the box, took out the picture of Rosa and Eddie on their wedding day, put it in a frame, and hung it on one of the shelves.

Chapter 8

Rosie carried the small wooden rose in her pocket and was never without it. Whenever she thought of her mother, she would put her hand in her pocket and touch the token of love. Whenever she felt anxious or tired, the token gave her comfort and strength.

Following that day when she found her father's love for her, she spent many happy days and evenings in his company. Sometimes Rosie walked out with her Pa learning new routes and places to go to sell sprigs of heather and pieces of lace. He always taught her to be careful about where she went and to trust her instinct. They still went to fairs, but times were changing and more and more travellers were beginning to settle or stay in places for longer periods. Some were getting rid of their wagons and buying motorised vans.

Travelling women tended to sell pegs, china pottery, handmade flowers, and lace for trimming clothes or tableware. Some, gifted with the sight, would tell a fortune for a piece of silver. She knew her Granny Mary had the gift of the sight, for she had heard the other women whispering about it, but she didn't think that she had it.

She once heard them whisper about a time when she was just a baby. They said something about her being sick and Granny Mary was running in the rain to get help when an American gentleman riding by in a fancy carriage refused to stop.

She didn't know any more about it, but she did hear one of the women saying something about never crossing the Mither and she knew they were talking about her granny.

Her granny always told her to trust her instincts. She said if she felt that something was good then it was, but if she felt that something was bad then she should run as fast as her legs would carry her. Her granny was funny with her sayings.

The men folk worked the fields gathering tatties, pulling turnips, or picking fruits. Others would have grinding carts, and they would go around houses and farms sharpening tools. Smithing, breeding, training, and trading horses, lurchers and terriers and sometimes ferrets for hunting was a popular way to earn money.

Eddie's business, building quality wagons for newlyweds and for travellers who were doing well, was growing. His reputation as an artisan brought him many orders, enough that he could enlist the help of men within his own group. He used the shed that he had built on the land purchased from the farmer several years before, and before long he was able to buy more land from the same farmer.

Occasionally he would meet up with Arab traders who brought Persian rugs to the UK hoping to make their fortune. Eddie would buy a cartload and then pass them on to others in his community for a small profit, and they then sold the rugs from door to door. He made time to travel to the fairs at Musselburgh, St James fair in Kelso, and Appleby Horse Fair often taking Mary and young Rosie with him.

Rosie was growing more beautiful by the day and more like her mother in many ways. Even her voice reminded him of Rosa, sometimes he would hear Rosie chatting or singing, and it was as though Rosa was by his side. Rosie's responsibility was to help her granny keep the home clean and cook the food.

There might be fish or meat caught using nets, ferrets, catapults, or dogs and sometimes they would cook squirrels, hedgehogs, hares, and pheasant. When they needed to, they could buy or trade meat from a local butcher, or sell him any excess that they caught. They made flavoured drinks and jams, from fruits that they had gathered, or they would preserve them for future use. They made natural remedies from herbs and stored some in jars or brown paper bags to flavour their food.

When there was time to spare, they would go from door to door selling fancy lace for collars, or trims and wooden clothes pegs. Some homes treated them kindly, but others treated them with scorn and disrespect, throwing things at them and calling them names.

"Why do they call us Tinkers Granny?"

"Its jist their ignorance lass. They think they're insultin' us, but 'tinker' comes from the tinkling' noise that's made from the pots an' pans we sell hangin from the carts."

Over time, Rosie knew where to avoid and where she would be able to earn a penny or two.

As time passed, with the onset of arthritis, Mary was finding it harder to go from door to door selling their wares so, Rosie went on her own. Rosie kept to areas close to where they were camped, so that she could help her granny by fetching and carrying water for cleaning or cooking, and wood for their fire.

Life was beginning to return to normal, but it would never be the same as it had been before the war. There were houses, where before the war there were fields, and factories had sprouted up. By 1923 motorised buses were becoming more common and there were many more cars on the roads and further afield. Everything seemed to be noisier, dirtier and rushed, although for Rosie and the rest of her community, they tried to maintain the old ways.

Mary at fifty-one looked much older than her years. The loss of Rosa and John had added lines to her face. Arthritis troubled her daily and made getting about a painful trial. Her long white hair dressed in a middle parting with pleats on either side was partially concealed under a black crocheted shawl. In her younger days, bright colours were her choice, but since the death of Rosa she had always worn black.

Her skin was weather beaten and lined with wrinkles, but in Rosie's eyes, it was the loveliest of faces.

"Have ye everything ye need Granny?"

"Aye lass Ah'm fine, why dae ye ask?"

"Ah'm gonnae head o'er the Glasgow Bridge this morning. See if Ah can sell some heather an' lace tae folk goin' tae work. Maybe go as far as Kinning Park. Ma baskets fu' o stuff Ah've been makin'."

"Aye, folk might be thinkin' o things tae buy. Ye could take some jams if there's spare."

"Next time granny, ma baskets full tae burstin."

"You mind yir self lass and don't trust a face cause it's smiling at ye."

Rosie was smiling as she leant over and kissed granny on the forehead and went out the door. Her granny had lots of saying like that…

"Keep yer hon on yer ha'penny an' don't gie it away for a penny"

"Ne're shed a cloot tae May is oot."

"Gang wi' the craws git shot doon wi' the craws."

Rosie amused herself laughing and thinking of her granny's sayings as she walked from Fleshers Haugh at Glasgow Green along the banks of the River Clyde.

"Whit's for ye'll no go by ye!"

"Lang may yer lum reek."

"Dinnae teach yer Granny tae suck eggs."

Her basket was packed with small sprigs of heather tied with string into little bunches and pieces of lace were rolled into yard long lengths. Her basket was full, but light enough that she had one hand free to hold out a piece of lace or a bunch of heather to people she passed along the way.

When she wasn't offering something, she would put her hand in her pocket, and finger the little wooden rose token and make a wish for the next person to buy from her. She made her way towards the Glasgow Bridge, and was glad to see that it was teeming with people crossing the bridge to the city and going the other way to the docks and warehouses that ran along the Clyde.

"Lucky white heather a penny a bunch."

"Lucky white heather."

"A bit o' lace for yer missus?"

Not many on the bridge took her up on her offer.

"In too much of a hurry." she thought as she gazed over the parapet and watched people boarding the King Edward steamer. In those days, the Clyde was a hive of activity with steamers, puffers, and small cargo ships from the recently formed Burns and Laird line.

Chapter 9

She didn't have much luck on the bridge as people jostled each other hurrying to wherever they were going. Tramcars and horse drawn dray wagons from the bonded warehouses at Port Dundas, all fought for room to move back and forth. Over the bridge, she headed towards Paisley Road to the tenements in Kinning Park. The tenements were grimy, and some of the children made a fool of her and called her names, but she always managed to sell a thing or two there.

She went from door to door; always staying on the ground floor level of the tenements, and eventually she came to St James Street. She hated the dark dingy closes and the smell that hung in the air. She could never understand why people would want to walk through filth to get to their own door. If she and her granny lived there, they would clean every day and the close would smell fresh and sweet.

There was a man who lived in one of the ground floor flats who always bought a bit of lace for his wife, and he always gave her an extra penny or two for her trouble. Sometimes he offered her a drink of lemonade or a sweetie. She thought he was a bit "away in the heed," because he always laughed when he opened the door to her and announced,

"Have ye come to see Mr James of St James Street?"

She always played the game and said,

"Aye, Ah've come to sell Mr James of St James Street a bit o' lace for yer missus,"

"Will ye come in lass n have a sip o' lemonade?" he said.

Her Granny Mary always told her,

"Never cross the front door when sellin yer wares as ye cannae trust a buddy 'specially if they're nae yer ane kind".

She had never gone in before, but she was tired from her long trek and her throat was dry from speaking to people. Her granny's words forgotten, Rosie stepped over the threshold of Mr James of St James Street's house.

The room was dark, dingy, and dirty, it didn't look as though as though a woman lived there and Rosie wondered why he had been buying the lace. She glanced round the room, the curtains on the window were closed tight, and there was a stale smell filling her nose. Two armchairs sat either side of a dirty fireplace and she noticed a fat man sitting on one of them. He staring at her with a look on his face that made her stomach turn.

By the window stood a wooden trunk with handles on either side and leather straps that wrapped around it fastened with buckles. She felt afraid and didn't know what to say or do.

"Where's yer missus?" she asked, panic beginning to burn in her chest.

Both men laughed at her. She felt Mr James put his hands on her shoulders, and she turned with a start and backed away from him, but the table in the middle of the room stopped her.

"Dinnae dae that Mr James."

"Awe come lass, Ah'm sure ye know whit's whit." he said menacingly, moving closer to her.

She tried to slip past him, but he was between her and the door.

"Come on ye can have a bit o' fun now a bonnie lass like you, Ah've waited a long time for ye."

She screamed as he lunged for her forcing his mouth on hers and splitting her lip. She saw the fat man coming towards them and for a minute, she thought he was going to help her.

"Ah'll hawd her doon." She heard him say.

She tried to scream again as she fought them off like wildcat. She kicked out and bit as Mr James held his big thick hands over her mouth and nose to stifle her screams, but he was choking the life from her. She fought, kicked, and struggled, and felt something hard and heavy hit her on her head. Bit by bit, her strength disappeared, and the last coherent thought she had was

"Granny"

"Ya' crazy bastart' whit have ye done she's deed!" Mr James said to the fat man standing over Rosie's body.

"She shouldha' kept quiet then."

"Whit are wi' gonnae dae?"

"Get her clathes aff and empty her poackets an' that basket. Burn awe that in the fire. Its nearly teatime, the factories are emptyin' and it'll be gettin' dark. We'll stick her in the trunk and dump her in the Clyde."

"Are ye effin' crazy man, how are we supposed to get her tae the Clyde in that trunk wi'oot onybody seein' us."

"They'll think wur sailors gone back tae the boat. They'll no mind us among the melee comin' an' goin' fae their work. They might see us, but they widnae' think we were putting a body in the Clyde. Hurry up gie me a hawn." He laughed

The fat man began to burn the lace and heather in the fireplace, and at the bottom of Rosie's basket, he found the money from her sales and counted it out. "Three shillin's, that'll be ma pay for the dirty work ye huv me daein'," he said, as he put the handfuls of pennies and halfpennies in his pocket.

Mr James was stripping Rosie's clothes off.

"Awe whit a shame she's deed, we couldha had a nice bit o' fun wi' that yin."

The fat man took Rosie's clothes and went through her pockets and found the little wooden rose, "Whit aboot this, dae ye want it?" he asked.

"Naa, Burn it wi' the rest."

The fat man looked at the carving of the rose on the face of the wooden token and slipped it into his pocket. Together they picked Rosie's lifeless body and put her into the trunk then fastened down the straps.

"Whit are wi' gonnae say if anybody asks us whit where dayin."

W'ull just say Ah'm ge'in ye a hawn back tae yer ship." Then he laughed again and said,

"We'll ask them tae gie us a hawn and then they'll no be very long in mindin' their ane business."

They carried the trunk between them along St James Street. They were only a few minutes walk from the Clyde, it was already growing dark, and the rain had started to fall. People were hurrying towards their homes, but no one bothered them. They crossed some spare ground to reach the spot that they wanted to dump the trunk and Rosie's remains.

"Ye ken this is tidal," said the fat man.

"Dae a look' stupit."

"Ah never said that, Ah'm jist remindin' ye."

"Well hurry up, get some o' these big stones an' we'll make sure it goes deep an' disnae move. As soon as it lands it'll sink in the silt."

Hurriedly they gathered boulders and put them in the trunk, and then they closed the lid on Rosie and fastened the straps again. They dragged the trunk to the edge of the Clyde, made sure there was no one around and together they heaved and pushed until the trunk slipped into its resting place. As they walked the fat man pulled his hankie from his pocket, and as he did so the little wooden token spilled out of his pocket and rolled away. Neither of the men even noticed it.

"Where did ye put that money ye found?"

"In ma poakit."

"Aye, well yer buyin, let's go for a pint."

And with that, they sauntered off to the nearest pub.

Chapter 10

Granny Mary had a bad feeling in her stomach and pains in her chest. She didn't know that she was suffering from angina. She looked at the old clock on the wall and then she rose to look out of the window of the wagon. It was raining hard, she knew a storm was brewing and she felt sick. She began to pace and tried to still her mind, but the feeling of dread grew in her.

She had avoided her gift of the sight for a long time and although it was still there it was weaker through lack of use, nevertheless her instincts were screaming at her that something bad was happening, and her worst fear was that Rosie was in trouble, serious trouble.

Suddenly there was a crash and the photograph of Rosa and Eddie fell off the shelf. She put her hand to her mouth and stood there staring as the tears began to course down her face. Slowly she moved to the photograph lying face down by the hearth. With difficulty, holding her shawl over her shoulders, she stooped to pick it up. Rosa's face on her wedding day looked back at her. The picture was undamaged, but the frame had broken beyond repair.

The pain in her heart worsened as the panic grew. She tried to still her fears, but deep down she knew there was something terribly wrong. She opened the door of her wagon and called to a neighbouring wagon.

"Bella, Bella come quick."

Bella came over, "Whit's up Mither?" she said using the term Mither as a sign of respect.

"Have ye taken bad?"

"Its Rosie, summat terrible has happened," she said clutching Bella's hand.

"Send somebody tae fetch oor Eddie an' the lads."

"But whit's happened, whit's happened?"

"Ah dinnae ken, but Ah know it's bad, fetch the men an' be quick. She shouldha been hame afore noo."

Eddie and the other men from the camp had gathered within the hour, and still there was no sign of Rosie.

"Where'd she go the day Granny?"

"Doon by the docks, maybe Clyde Street an' across the water."

The men huddled in a group and discussed the plan to search various areas. Some had bicycles, others horses, and they went off in different directions. Knocking on doors as they came to them or stopping folk in the street. The question was the same from all of them.

"Have ye seen oor lass, she goes by the name Rosie. Sellin' lace she was, maybe pegs. She's a pretty lass wi' long dark curly hair."

Some remembered seeing her in the past, some knew her by name, and some just shook their head and walked on disinterested. There were not so many people on the streets because of the weather, but they continued to search for hours. There were no phones to communicate with each other so at various points along the distance, between the camp and the search area, one of the men would wait so that a signal could be given if anyone found any sign of Rosie, or if she returned home.

All the women gathered together in and outside Eddie's wagon to give and seek comfort. She was one of their own and they would search until they found her. They searched all night, and finally in the early hours of the morning, Eddie and his cousin Tam went into the new Orkney Street Police Station. The duty constable looked up from his desk and eyed the men up and down contemptuously without saying a word.

"Ma lass is missin'," he said.

"What makes ye think she's missing."

"She never came home last night."

"And what age would this lass be," the constable said.

"She's jist turned sixteen," replied Eddie.

He saw the smirk on the constable's face.

"And is there a boyfriend missing as well?"

Tam quickly grabbed Eddie and held him back for he was about to punch the constable on the nose.

"She's a guid lass, there's nae boyfriend. Ah'm tellin' ye she's missin', she never came hame last night an' we've searched awe night for her."

"Wait a minute," the constable said, and left the desk and went through a door behind him into an office.

They could see him through the frosted glass as though he was talking to someone in the office, but when he came back, they could see through the door that the office was empty.

"The gaffer said leave it till tomorrow and if she's still not back come and see us."

They stared at each other for a few moments. Eddie and his cousin knew that the constable was lying, and the constable knew that they knew it, but it didn't matter a jot to him. In his mind, the missing tinker lassie had run off with a sweetheart.

"Come on Eddie," said Tam "We'll git nae help here."

He took Eddie by the arm. He could feel Eddie shaking with rage and frustration in his bones as he all, but dragged him out of the station. In those days when a person was missing, it was unlikely that there would be any action taken until twenty-four to forty-eight hours had passed unless they were vulnerable.

At that time a sixteen-year-old gypsy girl was not considered vulnerable.

They walked up Broomloan Road and onto Paisley Road West stopping people as they went, asking them if they had seen Rosie. They continued on making their way towards the bridge over the River Clyde heading back to where they were camped.

Eddie's head was down, his shoulders slumped in despair, and Tam didn't know what to say to him. What can you say to someone when you yourself think the worst has happened? Just at the corner of St James Street Eddie's shoe made contact with something on the pavement and it rolled to the gutter, he walked on for a moment, and then he stopped dead in his tracks.

"Whit is it man?" Tam said.

"Whit was that, where did it go?" he said as he turned sharply and started searching and there it was, the wooden rose that he had carved for his Rosa and passed to his daughter Rosie when she was barely fourteen. She had carried it ever since.

"Aw' naw!" he cried as he knelt by the kerb, "Naw, naw, naw, she's somewhere here," he said, clutching the wooden rose as though it were a lifeline. It was early morning, and while some would be getting ready to go to work others were still asleep, but that didn't matter to Tam and Eddie. They turned into St James Street and started banging on doors and shouting to people.

"Away wi' ye afore we call the polis, tinkers, bloody cheek," some said.

They went to every door on every floor in each tenement and finally arrived at Mr James's door.

"Aye, Ah've seen her before, but no for a while," he said "But Ah'll watch for her an' tell her yer lookin'"."

Finally, they made their way back to the camp to find that about a hundred of their community had arrived to help with the search and were waiting for their return. Such is the nature of the travelling community that yes, they celebrated together, but they also gathered to help each other when one of their own was in trouble or needed support.

Tam shook his head discretely to the gathered men, warning them to give him a bit of time before they spoke to him. They separated as he walked between their ranks, some reaching out to touch his shoulder or arm as he passed with his head down and his face drawn in anguish. The women stood and made way as he approached his wagon.

He stepped into the wagon and looked at Granny Mary. He couldn't speak and nor could she as he held out his hand to show her what he had found. Outside where the travellers had gathered, men women and children shivered as the keening grew louder and louder as Granny Mary wailed in her grief.

Some of the older women came in to comfort her, and Eddie went out to join the men who waited by the campfire. Someone put a bowl of soup in his hand and another set a whisky down beside him. He told them as best he could where they had looked and what they had found at St James Street. They decided that the men would gather at St James Street to begin the search again, and Eddie would go back to Orkney Street Police Station.

The following morning, while Eddie went back to Orkney Street Police Station almost one hundred travellers gathered around St James Street and began banging on doors. This caused some alarm, such an unusual event, that runners were sent to Orkney Street to fetch the police.

The runners arrived at the police station while Eddie was trying to get them to look for Rosie. The sergeant was more sympathetic than the constable had been the day before and he reprimanded him out of earshot of the people who had now gathered in the station.

Communications were poor then, but the sergeant listened to Eddie's report of where he thought Rosie had been and where they had since searched. He told the sergeant where he had found Rosie's token and the significance of it.

The sergeant explained to Eddie that he would notify other stations at the start of the next shift so that constables could search various locations.

There were no mobiles in those days or biro pens. Constables would make notes in their notebooks with a pencil and the radios that they did have merely clicked rather than allowing the opportunity for speech. The sergeant organised a search and instructed officers to go from door to door and leave no stone unturned. The search went on for several days but it was fruitless. The constable who had been on duty on that first day had wasted valuable time, and any trail had since gone cold.

Chapter 11

People that had come to help stayed at the camp for more than a week, but they had to return to their families and their daily life. Day after day, week after week, Eddie searched for Rosie. He searched from Glasgow Green, through the city and over the Clyde. He searched in Kinning Park and as far as Govan, but never found a trace. Some days he walked the banks of the Clyde. He was sure that Rosie would never have ventured onto the docks, but he even searched there. Some days Tam would go with him, but on other days, he insisted on being by himself. He was a constant visitor pestering the life of the sergeant at Orkney Street, but nothing changed.

Each evening he would return to the camp worn out and heart weary. At first folk would look at him as he arrived back and ask

"Any news Eddie?" and he would just shake his head sadly.

He would climb the steps to the wagon only to find Granny Mary sitting staring off into space in silent agony.

Most nights he would lie awake and on the nights that he slept, he would find himself tortured by nightmares. Often he would rise in the middle of the night and he would hear Granny Mary whimpering in a fretful sleep.

Granny Mary was failing fast; her legs wouldn't hold her, and her grief was more than she could bear. She had lost the will to live and was fading away before everyone's eyes.

Bella and some of the other mothers took turns every day looking after Mary, but no amount of encouragement would make her eat a proper meal or leave the wagon. Bella pleaded with her to let her send for the doctor, but Mary demanded that she be left alone. By November, Mary's condition had deteriorated and one morning Bella went looking for Eddie.

"Ye better come Eddie, Ah'm that feart aboot the Mither. The pains in her chest are bad an' she'll no let me call a doctor."

Eddie stopped grooming his horses, not that he was even aware of what he was doing, because his mind was on his daughter. He went into the wagon and there was Granny Mary, white as a sheet, lying on the couch against the wall, her face drawn with pain.

"Ah have seen her ye know, an' whit Ah have seen is terrible, Ah'll never rest until she's found. A lass'll fin' her ye know, but no for a while yet, no for a long while."

The tears coursed down her wrinkled skin. Eddie sat on the couch at her side and held her bony hand. Grief touched him again and stuck a knife in his heart.

"Ah'm gonnae send for the doctor Granny."

"Nah, nah dae nothin' oh the kind. Let me go, let me be wi' ma Johnny, Rosa, an' Rosie. Ah cannae bear this pain o livin'. Let me go laddie, let me go. Take me outside, Ah want to look at the sky wan last time afore Ah go."

Travelling folk preferred to die outside, and those that had gathered to wait in respect had had prepared a bed supported on a trestle. Eddie went to the door of the wagon and looked at Tam who was nearest to him. Tam nodded and a few of the men came into the wagon to support Eddie as he carefully and lovingly lifted Mary and took her outside. Together they laid her down on the bed and covered her with a clean white blanket.

The November air was still as Eddie stayed by her side holding her hand and remembering happier times. Remembering how she had looked as a younger woman when he was courting Rosa. How could so much pain come to someone who had been so kind and loving to him? Friends at the camp gathered sensing that her time was near and none had a dry face. All had memories of Mary and things she had done to help them; she made them laugh when they were down in the dumps, and made them potions from herbs that made them well when they were sick. Aye, everyone loved Mary. Few remembered her darker side, for mostly that side of her character had calmed after she and Johnny had started courting.

As they gathered there, standing guard in her final minutes a robin landed nearby. All heads turned for all had seen it, and as they watched Mary gave one last sigh, one last breath, and the essence of her was gone. She passed quietly away and as she did, the robin took flight singing its mournful, warbling, song. Eddie kissed her forehead and said

"Away then Mither and find yer Johnny, and then the pair o' ye find my Rosa an' ma Rosie. Tell them Ah'll be joinin' them soon enough."

The women lit candles, put them into glass jars, and placed them around the trestle to light Mary's way to the afterlife. Someone went for the undertaker and before long Mary was taken away to be looked after and prepared for her final resting place. She was to be dressed in her best clothes and jewellery, for there was no daughter or granddaughter to inherit. They would bury Mary beside Rosa at Janefield Cemetery in the Gallowgate, until then, the men would stand vigil at the funeral parlour.

Everything and everyone drew to a standstill as four hundred mourners turned up to pay their respects. The solemn procession walked behind the horse drawn hearse, and the four white horse's bridles and headbands were dressed with fancy plumage and brass hangings. The air was still and quiet in spite of the number of people and all that could be heard was the clip clop of the horse's hooves.

After the funeral, the women of the camp provided food for everyone, and they held a grand wake to share stories and memories of loved ones who had passed. Some of the old mither's from other families whispered about Mary's curse, and said that the American's family was already suffering and none could stop the curse now that Mary was gone.

It was several days before people went back to their own camps or homes, and when they were gone Eddie spoke to Tam. In his heart, Eddie knew that his lovely Rosie was gone from him forever and the only consolation that he had was that she was with her Ma, her Granny, and her Papa and that neither of them would be as lonely as he was.

Tam had hardly left Eddie's side since Rosie disappeared. Anyone who saw them would think that they were brothers instead of cousins because they looked so like each other. The main difference was that Tam had red hair where Eddie's hair was jet black.

"Ah'm goin' on the road for a bit Tam, look after things, ye know where everything is."

"Ah'll come wi' ye man."

Eddie put his hand on Tams shoulder and looked into his tear-filled eyes.

"Ah'll be better ma self. You bide here an' look after the wagons, some need finishin', an' the horses. It's aw yours' man."

Tam was choked with grief and could do nothing to help Eddie other than what he asked.

"It'll be here when ye come back."

Eddie patted Tam on the back and said, "Aye man, Ah know."

He started to walk away from Tam, but Tam grabbed him and put his arms around him holding his cousin and best friend for a moment and then the two men parted. Eddie walked away without looking back. He drove his wagon away from the camp towing a trailer behind him. When others asked him where he was going he replied that he was going on a journey and told no one of his destination.

He drove the wagon along the shores of Loch Lomond and onwards to begin the climb over the 'Rest and be Thankful' following the routes that he had taken to his wedding to Rosa sixteen years ago. He turned into Gleann Mor and when he found a suitable derelict spot, he unhitched the horses and the trailer. He dragged the trailer away to one side, took the horses, and hitched them to the trailer. He went back to the wagon, stood for a moment looking inside the home he had created for Rosa then he took some paper, lit it, and threw it inside before turning his back and walking away from the burning wagon.

He continued on his journey with little more than the clothes he stood in, the bedding and the pot or two that he had in the trailer.

He climbed the hill to the Tinkers Heart and there he stood gazing around him, looking at the loch below and the hills and mountains beyond. His thoughts travelled back to the journey that his life had been on, and he thought back to the day he had watched his Rosa, climbing the hill towards him with her Father on their wedding day.

He put his hand in his pocket and drew out the little wooden rose that he had carved twenty-four years before. He held it in his hand as he lay down in the Tinkers Heart, and there he stayed in the middle of the heart and wept until he had no tears left, until he was empty. Eddie was never seen again, but he was remembered for a long, long, time.

Part Two Present Day

Chapter 12

Alina Jones listened to her mother's voice as the answering machine recorded the message.

"Dad and I are going to take a drive down the coast and wondered if you would like to come with us. If we don't hear back from you within the hour, we will just go ourselves. I hope you can come."

Alina's face was blotchy and her eyes were red from crying after having an argument with her husband James. She wanted to go with her Mum and Dad, just to be with them and enjoy their company, but she knew that they would immediately know that something was wrong, and she just didn't want to talk about it.

She thought about calling them back and making excuses, but her parents knew her too well, and the minute her Mum heard her voice she would know something was wrong. She hated that she was having problems, and hated her parents knowing about them more.

She knew her Mum would ask her what was wrong and she didn't want to go through an explanation of the argument that she had with James. Two or three times she reached for the phone and changed her mind. What had she become she wondered, who was this dominated woman inside her skin?

James had gone off to his work in the city, he had a career in savings and investments, and they had a nice three bedroom detached home, garden, and a double garage for his and her cars. There was money in the bank that they could afford to spend on holidays, nice clothes, and small luxuries, but things were not as good as they could be.

More often than not, he came home late, missed planned dinners or birthday celebrations, and sometimes even cancelled things at the last minute because of business meetings. This had led to Alina feeling left out and lonely, and although she could have invited friends over to keep her company, James disliked her friends. It was easier to comply with James than argue over it and gradually she lost touch with them. She went upstairs to her bedroom, to lie on her bed and let her mind drift back over their life together.

Alina had worked full time in banking and she remembered the day that tall, dark, handsome James Jones had come to the branch to meet with a customer. He was wearing a navy pin stripe suit, a white shirt, and a navy and white diagonal striped silk tie. All the female tellers glanced at each other, making subtle eye movements to indicate their attraction to the handsome newcomer.

She was giving him a second look as he was giving her one, their eyes met and for her that was it. Cupid's arrow had struck her, and she did not refuse when later, after he had left the branch, someone called her to the telephone.

"Alina Webster," she said, assuming it was a customer. "How can I help you?"

"I wondered if you would like to join me for dinner?" a male voice said.

"Excuse me!" she replied, puzzled. "Who is this?"

"It's James Jones, just call me JJ."

"How do you know my name?"

"It's on the badge pinned to your blouse. I noticed your long dark hair and pretty blue eyes too," he laughed.

"I don't even know you," she replied.

She was smiling when she recognised who was calling her and she knew that she would go for dinner with him; however, she didn't want to appear to be too keen. She whispered to her colleagues and told them about the call from the handsome stranger. She remembered how her work mates had laughed and teased her.

That was the beginning of a wonderful romance with JJ; he took her for dinner to fancy restaurants, bought her flowers, and surprised her with weekends away and gifts. She was twenty-two and being swept off her feet, but in spite of that, neither her parents nor her friends liked him. Her mother said he was smarmy, whatever that meant. Alina could not see any fault in him whatsoever, and six months after they first met, on her twenty-third birthday, he proposed to her by taking her to a house in Bearsden with an 'Under Offer' sign outside. He had suggested that he was 'giving it the once over' for a friend.

"What do you think?" he asked as they walked around the outside.

"It's lovely," she said.

"Come on inside," he said taking her hand and leading her up the three steps to the front door. He took her into the front room and there in the middle was a small circular table with two chairs either side; on the table were roses, a bottle of champagne, and two glasses.

"Oh my goodness," she said mystified. "That's' an unusual way to dress a house for viewing."

Alina's face was a picture to behold as she looked at the table and its bounty. JJ laughed and said, "Sometimes you are so innocent Alina; I put these things together for you."

As she turned to look at him in surprise, JJ promptly knelt in front of her and said, "Marry me Alina, and this will be our home. All I have to do is sign the missives."

In his hand, he was holding a red velvet ring box with a beautiful solitaire diamond ring inside.

There was one small niggle in the back of her mind. As they entered the house, she noticed that the number was sixteen and for Alina, that was not a good number. She had studied Tarot cards and numerology and occasionally read for her friends. The sixteenth card in the Major Arcana of Tarot cards is the Tower. Alina knew that 'The Tower' represented disaster, loss of control and grief. She shrugged off her feelings and allowed the thrill of the moment to over ride her doubt. She should have known better.

The next couple of months were a whirlwind of planning for her wedding, but JJ had no family and a quiet wedding, was what JJ wanted. Now that she reminisced, she realised that JJ always got what he wanted. Her parents were disappointed, especially her mother who, like every mother thought about a daughter's wedding day.

Her parents had no living relatives so it wasn't as though they were offending anyone; at least, that was JJ's argument. In the end they had a quiet wedding at Gretna Green with only her parents, JJ's friend Bob, acting as best man, and Alina's best friend Sheila acting as maid of honour. She knew her parents were disappointed, but in spite of their disappointment, they did their best to support her wishes.

She realised that everything in the past three years of married life had been what JJ wanted, and that she had become complacent and agreeable, even resigning from her job so that she would be at his 'beck and call'.

Chapter 13

Alina was in a deep exhausted sleep dreaming that she was trapped somewhere, and a loud noise was alerting her to danger, but she couldn't escape. Clarity interrupted her nightmare, and she realised her mobile phone was ringing. She looked at the display as she answered.

"Mum," she said, and a man's voice answered her.

"Hello, who is this?" she said, "And why are you using my mother's phone?"

"Is this Alina, your name is the last number called on this phone, I take it that this is your mothers phone?" he questioned.

"Yes, did you find it?"

"Well no, not exactly. I'm Constable Riley, you see your parents have been in an accident. I take it your mother was travelling with your father."

"Yes, yes, oh God what's happened to them, are they alright?"

"I have been given this number to contact next of kin and let you know that they have been taken to The Vale of Leven Hospital. Do you know where that is?"

"Are they alright?" she almost screamed at him.

"I don't have any other information other than where they are. I am sorry," he said.

She grabbed her bag and her car keys, threw the phone into her bag, and raced out of the house. Her MG sports car was in the garage and she fumbled, dropping her keys as she tried to open the 'up and over' garage door. She did not even stop to close it before she reversed out of her driveway. She took the Duntocher Road then picked up the A82 to Alexandria. Thirty minutes later, she was at the main reception desk of The Vale of Leven Hospital.

"My parents are here, I had a call from the police to say they had been involved in an accident, Mr and Mrs Webster, can I see them please, tell me where they are please?" the words rushed out of her mouth.

"Oh, one moment please," the receptionist said.

She left Alina waiting there as she went through an internal door. Alina waited anxiously. A few moments later, the receptionist came back.

"Someone will come for you in a moment if you would like to just wait here."

"Are you Miss Webster?" the receptionist asked her.

"No, Mrs James."

A nurse appeared through the internal door and the receptionist turned and said to her.

"This is Mr and Mrs Webster's daughter Mrs James"

The nurse came around from the reception area and smiled kindly at Alina.

"Is someone with you?" the nurse asked taking Alina by the arm and leading her away from the main area and along a corridor.

Alina turned and looked at the nurse, and said firmly, "Look I don't need anyone with me; I just want to see my parents please."

"Just in here," the nurse said, and led her into a small room and closed the door.

The hair stood up on the back of Alina's neck.

"What's going on, I want to see my Mum and Dad."

"I understand," the nurse said, "please sit down a minute."

"I don't want to sit down thank you, you are not listening to me, I just want to see my Mum and Dad, and I want to see them right now."

"I am so very sorry to tell you ..."

Before the nurse could say another word Alina heard a keening sound, getting louder and louder, then she realised that the sound was coming from her. In her heart, she had known this was serious by the way the receptionist looked at her, and by how the nurse behaved, but she did not want to accept the fact that her parents were dead. She doubled over with her face in her hands.

"Oh God I should have been with them. I wish I had been with them. I didn't pick up the phone. I will never forgive myself."

Her tears flowed endlessly and the pain in her heart was unbearable.

The nurse held her in her arms as she sobbed.

"Is there someone you can call?"

"Yes, I will call my husband."

"Let me get you a cup of tea, I will be back in a minute."

She dialled JJ's number and it cut off immediately. She tried again, same thing. She called his office and his assistant answered.

"Can I speak to JJ please? Tell him it's his wife."

"I am very sorry Mrs James, he isn't in the office at the moment," she replied.

"Do you know where he is or when he will be back?"

"I'm sorry no, I don't know when he will be back, he just said that he had a meeting, have you tried his mobile?"

"I have to speak to him urgently. Just ask him to call me as soon as you hear from him."

"I will," said the assistant.

The nurse came in with a cup of tea, some milk, and some sugar.

"Is your husband coming Mrs James?"

"No, at least I don't know, I couldn't get a hold of him, I left a message."

"What happened to my parents?"

"There is a policeman waiting outside to see you. Do you want me to give you a few more minutes?"

"No, I want to know what happened and I want to see my parents."

The nurse went out of the room and came back a few moments later accompanied by a police officer.

"What happened to my parents?" she asked.

"It looks as though your father had a heart attack, and the car veered off the road and down an embankment. Your mother died on impact. No one else was involved."

He paused between each statement trying to break the news gently.

"I'm sorry for your loss Mrs James."

Alina broke down again and covered her face with her hands.

"I don't know what I am supposed to do now," she cried.

The nurse stepped forward, crouched in front of Alina, and took Alina's hands in hers. "We have someone here who can help you, try to drink some more of your tea."

The police officer gave Alina a card with his name and contact details before he left, and Alina tried to call JJ once more, but his mobile was still off.

"Would you like me to take you to the hospital chapel?" the nurse asked.

"I would really just like to see my parents," Alina replied.

"Let's go along to the chapel first; I will take you to see your parents as soon as they are prepared for you."

"I don't understand?"

"They will be taken to a special viewing room."

"Are they badly injured, I mean are they marked?"

"No, they will look just as you remember them."

"No they won't, they are dead. How can that be just as I remembered them?"

The nurse accompanied Alina to the hospital chapel and left her there, telling her that she would come back in ten minutes or so. Alina sat it the little chapel her face wet with tears.

"Please forgive me Mum, I didn't speak to you on the phone because I knew that you would know that I was upset, and I didn't want to talk about it or worry you and spoil your day. Maybe you would still be here if I had answered the phone."

She thought about her Dad, at sixty-five he was seven years older than her Mum was. He had looked older since he had suffered a minor heart attack a couple of years before. When he walked, his steps were shallow, not dragging his feet exactly, but not as sprightly as they had been. He was more stooped than usual and as deaf as a post.

She thought back to times before she was married and remembered the way he would look at her with a twinkle in his eye and a half smile on his face. She would smile back at him and it was as though they shared a secret or a joke that no one else knew about, and then they would laugh at nothing and go off together to the local pub for a game of pool.

Her Mum would look on fondly at the pair of them. She had kept her slim figure and always took care of her appearance. She aged gracefully, not showing her grey hair so much because of her natural blonde colouring. She wasn't vain, she just liked to look nice so she visited her hairdresser every six weeks or so and liked to wear nice clothes. Ronnie, her Dad, loved her dearly.

When they were going out together, more often than not, her father would be waiting for her mother to get ready, and as she appeared, he would say, "Ah there she is, my glamorous Beverly." Of course, at all other times he and her friends just called her Bev. Alina loved her Mum deeply, but she was a 'Daddy's Girl' at heart.

"Oh Daddy what am I going to do without you and Mum?"

Part of her realised that though the loss for her was terrible and almost impossible to bear, her parents would not have to suffer the loss of one before the other.

Alina had been interested in the pagan path before her marriage, but JJ was scornful whenever she brought the subject of faith up and gradually her interest waned, but in her heart, she believed that there was a God and a Goddess.

She respected other faiths, but her own faith gave her the comfort of knowing that her parents would be reborn in another life, and that they would probably be soul mates forever until the end of time.

She knelt in front of the altar, and prayed. She asked for help to bear this terrible ordeal. She asked that her parent's spirits, wherever they were, would find safe passage to wherever the afterlife was. She rose and went to a three-tiered stand that had receptacles for T light candles.

She wondered if the lit candles that were already there represented loved ones who had died at the hospital today. She took two new candles and touched the wick to the flame of a lit candle. She lit one for her mother and another for her father, and wished that their memory would always burn brightly in her heart.

When the nurse came back, Alina followed her through a maze of corridors, the sound of their footsteps echoing in the cold silence. Eventually they came to the viewing rooms. As they entered, the nurse paused and asked Alina if she was ready. Alina nodded and the nurse took her through the next door, and there were her parents, lying side by side on two trolleys. A white sheet covered them both to the neck.

"They look as though they are sleeping."

Silent tears fell as she looked at them. The nurse left her to say her goodbyes, and Alina slowly walked forward to stand between her parents.

"This is where I spent most of my life, between Mum and Dad, holding their hands, going places together," she thought to herself. "I have no one now."

She reached over and kissed her mother's cold lips and her tears dripped onto her mother's cheeks.

"Don't cry my baby girl, don't cry." She heard her mother's words in her mind and in her heart.

She reached over to her father and rested her head on his chest and her arm over his head and she stroked his hair. "Oh Daddy, don't leave me." She cried. Memories of happy times came flooding back and she knew then that these precious memories would be all she had to hold onto.

The nurse had told her to take as much time as she needed and she told her to press a buzzer, indicating where it was, when she was ready. When Alina had said her goodbyes, she buzzed the nurse, who returned and took her back to the family room where she was introduced to Mrs Evans from family support.

Mrs Evans held Alina's hand in hers as she said

"I am so terribly sorry for your loss. I'm here to help you with some of the things that you will need to do over the next five days."

"Thank you," said Alina numbly.

"Come and sit by me," said Mrs Evans as she drew Alina towards a table and chairs that were set off to one side of the room. She had a folder full of paperwork on the table, and as she was about to open it Alina stopped her.

"I know you mean well and are just doing your job, but I'm afraid I can't do this right now. I just want to go home. Can't I take it with me and work through it on my own?"

"Yes of course you can, actually I have your parent's belongings here too," she said as she handed Alina the folder. There were two large carrier bags, she carried one, and Mrs Evans carried the other as she led Alina to the main exit of the hospital. Alina opened the boot of her car and placed the bags inside. Mrs Evans took Alina's hand and held it for a moment between her hands.

"This has been a terrible blow for you Mrs James. You may want to see your doctor if you feel as though you are not coping."

"Thank you, you have been very kind," Alina replied, as she stepped into her car and placed the folder on the passenger seat.

Chapter 14

It was almost four in the afternoon before Alina arrived back from the hospital. She unlocked her front door, went into the lounge, lay down on the sofa, and cried herself to sleep with the hospital folder lying on the floor by the sofa where she had dropped it. She had not had a return call from JJ, but she was so numb with grief that she did not even realise that he had not called her back.

It was nearer seven pm when his key in the door woke her from her exhausted sleep. She heard the thump of his briefcase as he dropped it in the hall, and then the tinkle of his keys landing on a glass bowl by the hallstand. She sat up trying to focus, wondering if she was still in an awful nightmare as the memory of what she had been doing earlier came back to her. Her long dark hair tumbled over her face and her eyes were puffy from crying all day.

"Look at the state of you." JJ said as he walked into the lounge undoing his tie and kicking off his shoes.

"Where have you been?"

"Where do you think I have been? I have been working. Have you been lying there all day?" He said.

"Why didn't you call me back?"

"I was busy and now I'm not, what did you want anyway."

"My parents were killed in a traffic accident on the Loch Lomond Road."

"Oh! Well that's not so good," he said as he made his way out of the room.

"I'm going for a shower; it's been a long day. Would you like me to pour you a brandy or something?"

She looked at him, and for the first time she really saw that there was no substance to him whatsoever. Was that his support? *Well that's not so good'* did he really just say that? She questioned herself as she went up to their bedroom and put her pyjamas and a change of clothes into a bag. She went to the shower, reached in, and turned off the water.

"What the hell are you doing?" he shouted angrily "I'm getting ready to go out."

"And I am going to spend the night at my parent's house. I have too many things to do and it would be easier from there. I will be back sometime tomorrow or maybe the next day."

"Fine, whatever, I can fend for myself for a couple of days. Make sure that you take your mobile in case I need to speak to you," he said indifferently, as he put the water on and turned his back to her. She looked at him in disgust.

"Selfish B," she thought to herself. She would take her mobile, but she wouldn't answer if he called her. She was not spiteful by nature, but this was an entirely different scenario.

Her parents house was in nearby Milngavie, a mere ten minutes away, and she could easily have done what was necessary on a daily basis, but her need to be close to her parents in some way was great, and the lack of support from JJ just confirmed her desire to spend a night or two at her parent's house.

Unbeknown to Alina, JJ was rather pleased with her decision.

She had never noticed before, but the minute that she stepped through her parent's front door, she realised that she could smell them. She opened the hall cupboard and took out her Dad's scarf and the jacket her Mum used when she was pottering around the garden and she carried them upstairs to her parents' bedroom. She clutched them tightly to her chest as she lay down on their bed and breathed in their scent.

She tossed and turned unable to stop crying and around four am she got up and went downstairs to the kitchen to make herself a cup of tea and some toast. She took her snack back up to the bedroom and climbed into her parents' bed. The sick feeling in her stomach began to ease as she half-heartedly ate her toast and drank her tea. She lay back down and tried to think about what she had to do in the morning and she remembered the folder that Mrs Evans had given her; it was still in the car, but exhaustion overcame her and she drifted off into a deep sleep.

When she woke up, she looked around the room, puzzled for a moment. The reality of yesterday's events came flooding back. She dragged herself out of bed and went downstairs and into the kitchen. She put the kettle on to make coffee and then went out to her car to collect the folder, the bags from the hospital and her overnight bag. She made her coffee, took it through to the sitting room, and glanced at the wall clock; it showed seven am.

Everything she looked at evoked a memory. She had bought that clock for her father on one of his birthdays and she remembered him saying that every time he looked at it he would think of her. The tables had turned now and every time she would look at it; she would think of her Dad.

She curled up on the sofa, picked up the folder and took out the papers. Right at the very top of the papers was the death certificate signed by a doctor at the hospital. She was not aware of the tears until she realised she could not see through them to read. She noticed the date first. Her parents had died on the twenty second. The significance of the number twenty-two did not escape her attention. Twenty-two is the number that represents crossing a bridge to a new beginning. She wondered what this would mean for her and for her parents too.

She believed in an afterlife and imagined them in a beautiful garden, her father sitting on a comfortable deck chair reading a newspaper or simply watching and smiling at her mother as she pottered among the flowers. Wiping her eyes, she began to read the next lot of papers. The first page revealed the title,

"What to do after someone dies"

Get a medical certificate from a GP or hospital doctor to register the death.

Register the death within five days and request documents required for the funeral.

Arrange the funeral by yourself or employ a funeral director to arrange it you.

The next title was

"Gather the following documents and information."

National Insurance number

National Health Service number

Date and place of birth

Date of marriage or civil partnership (if appropriate)

Child Benefit number (if appropriate)

Tax reference number

Notify the family doctor

Contact the deceased person's solicitor and obtain a copy of the will or if there is no solicitor search the deceased papers to locate a will.

Begin funeral arrangements - you will need to check the will for any special request

If relevant, a completed form should be sent to the local Social Security or Jobs & Benefits office regarding the deceased's benefits (if appropriate)

The next title suggested

"Who else to contact"

Insurance Companies to notify them of the bereavement and cease any policy

Banks or building societies (and accountant if appropriate) to close any accounts

Mortgage provider to freeze payments and consider future options

Hire purchase or loan companies to advise them of the death

Credit card providers'/store cards to cancel cards and close accounts

Utilities and household contacts to advise them of the death and arrange for final readings

Landlord or local authority if they rented a property

Royal Mail, to re-direct mail

TV or internet companies to cancel contracts

Telephone and mobile phone companies to cancel contracts

Local councils

The employer (if appropriate)

The school, college, or university (if appropriate)

The relevant Tax Office

National Insurance Contributions Office (if appropriate

Child Benefit Office (if appropriate)

UK Identity and Passport Service, to return and cancel a passport

DVLA, to return any driving licence, cancel car tax, or return car registration
documents

Alina looked at the documents in dismay and wondered how she would be able to cope with everything that she had to do.

Chapter 15

Alina sat staring off into space numb with grief; she couldn't think straight and didn't know where to start and she didn't know how she was going to cope. Her Mum was a well-organised person and she knew that she kept paperwork in an antique bureau in the study. She decided that the bureau would probably be the best place to start.

Just as she was about to begin her search the telephone rang. Alina turned and looked at it and dreaded picking it up. For a moment, she wondered if it was JJ, and then realised that he would most likely call her mobile. She picked up the phone.

"Morning Bev, I saw your light on, fancy a quick breakfast coffee?" said her mother's best friend and next-door neighbour Nancy.

"Nancy it's not Mum, it's me Alina." The lump in her throat almost choked her.

"Sorry Alina, are you ok?"

Alina found it hard to talk, "Can you come round?" she asked,

"I'll be there in one minute"

Nancy called upstairs to her husband Davey.

"I think something's wrong next door Davey, I've just spoken to Alina, and she sounds upset. I'll give you a shout in a bit."

Alina went to open the back door; she knew her mother and her neighbour's habits and knew that Nancy would come to that door.

"Oh my God you look awful Alina, what's happened pet, where's your Mum, has something happened to your Dad?"

Alina could not speak, she turned and put the kettle on and began to make Nancy a coffee.

"Speak to me pet, what's happened?" She said as she took Alina by the arm and turned her around to face her. She saw the tears coursing down Alina's face and wrapped her arms around her.

"There, there now, come on pet, tell me what's wrong" They both went through to the sitting room and Nancy sat Alina down then sat beside her.

"Oh Nancy they are both gone."

"Gone what do you mean gone?"

"They were killed yesterday on the Lomond Road, they said that Dad had a heart attack and lost control of the car and Mum died by his side."

"Dear God." Nancy slumped back into the chair, the colour had drained from her face, and she held her hands to her mouth as though she was trying to hold back her grief at the loss of her dear friends.

"I spoke to them yesterday, they told Davey and I that they were going for a run in the car. Oh, my God I cannot believe they are gone. Davey will be shattered, let me call him round."

Nancy went to the back door, called to her husband to come round, and waited there to close the door behind him.

He knew by the look on her face that something was wrong.

"What's up?"

"It's terrible news Davey, Ronnie and Bev were killed in a car accident on the Lomond Road yesterday."

"Never!"

"Come through to the sitting room, Alina is in a state, she looks like she has not slept for a week."

As he entered the sitting room, Alina stood up and went to him. She had known them most of her life and it was easy for her to lay her head on Davey's shoulder as she sobbed.

"There there, pet, just you have a good cry." He fondly patted her back looking over her shoulder at his wife while trying to console Alina. Nancy stood with tears falling from her eyes.

"I don't know how I'm going to cope without them."

He shook his head sadly his eyes full of tears.

"Well, we'll help you all we can to get through these difficult days. Have you contacted anyone yet?"

"No, not yet."

"Right, it's early yet for contacting people so let's get some food into you before we start and Nancy and I will help you. When did you last eat girl, you look as though you are ready to drop and you cannot function on an empty stomach. Here sit on the sofa and put your feet up. Nancy make us some breakfast love and I will call the surgery. Dr Naven should be informed. I'll leave a message for the receptionist to phone here urgently."

He came back into the sitting room and spoke to Alina.

"Just you rest a bit and I'll give Nancy a hand in the kitchen."

Alina did as was suggested; she put her head back on the corner cushion, and closed her eyes as she listened to Davey speaking to Nancy about the call to the surgery. Dr Naven was Davey and Nancy's doctor as well as hers and her parents. She knew he would be shocked too.

Nancy was putting together scrambled eggs and toast. She was as familiar in Bev's kitchen as she was in her own, but moving around her friend's domain, touching things that she knew Bev and Ronnie would never touch again made her very sad and she cried while she went about her task.

Davey patted her shoulder and asked her, "What can I do to help love?"

"Just set a tray for Alina while I plate these eggs."

They took the food through to the sitting room; Alina sat up and Nancy put the tray on her lap and encouraged her to eat. After they had finished eating, Nancy asked Alina if the hospital had given her a death certificate.

"They gave me a whole pile of stuff; it's all here in this folder."

Nancy opened the folder and spread the contents on the coffee table.

"We should contact the undertaker and then insurance company."

"Davey, I remember Bev saying something about it all being arranged. I know she has papers somewhere."

"Mum would have kept anything like that in the bureau."

Nancy began to search through the bureau and found what she was looking for in the bottom drawer. It was no surprise to Nancy that Bev had left everything neat and tidy in a folder.

She had included both her and Ronnie's wills, contact details for their lawyer, the insurance company, and the funeral director.

"She has everything organised here Alina, Davey and I will start making phone calls. The next of kin has to hand the death certificate into the registry office so Davey will take you there this afternoon. I just need your Mum's mobile to get the numbers of people that we should call."

"The hospital gave me those two carrier bags with their clothes and things; it might be in one of them."

"Shall I take a look?"

"Please, I can't bear to open them."

"I'll take them through to the kitchen."

Nancy picked up the bags and carried them through. One bag had Ronnie's clothes and shoes in it. The other had Bev's clothes, shoes and her handbag. Inside the handbag was her mobile phone, her purse and Ronnie's wallet. There was a cellophane pouch, and in it were Ronnie's watch, and Bev's necklace and earrings. Nancy's heart flipped a beat because she had bought them for Bev last Christmas.

She gathered the clothes, shoes, and jewellery, took them upstairs and put them in the bottom of the wardrobe in their bedroom. She set Bev's jewellery and Ronnie's watch on the dressing table.

She thought of Alina's husband. He should have been by her side at this difficult time, but she expected that his appearance would be limited for, as she had agreed with Bev, he was a selfish man and thought of no one but himself. She and Davey would help Alina, through this; it was the least they could do.

Chapter 16

She looked around at the sea of faces, all gathered to bid farewell to her Mum and Dad. There were so many people there that she didn't recognise, but everyone came to her and offered their sympathies and condolences.

The funeral was over and she was numb and bereft. JJ had put in a late appearance and tried to pretend that he was being supportive, but she could see that he was only doing so for the sake of appearances. He had no sooner arrived than he was gone again, 'pressure of work' being his excuse. That fact embarrassed her more than anything did. He had done nothing to help or support her, and it was Nancy and Davey who had helped her to organise everything even though they were grieving too.

She had spoken to her parent's solicitor and her parents had left everything to her including the house, which was mortgage free. In the weeks following the funeral, with Nancy's help, she emptied cupboards, wardrobes, and drawers giving things to charities. She kept some of her mother's favourite pieces of furniture, like the antique bureau and a small gate leg table with matching chairs upholstered in deep red velvet.

She told Davey to help himself to anything that he wanted from her Dad's shed and garage, and she gave Nancy her Mum's collection of books. Davey helped her to arrange self-storage for the things that she wanted to keep.

She had hardly seen anything of JJ during that period and had to avoid Nancy's questions about where he was and why he was not helping her. She made excuse after excuse often, lying to hide the humiliation that she felt about his lack of support.

Finalising her parent's estate and dealing with all the legalities that this involved took up most of her time. More often than not by the time she got home, he had already been home and had gone out again only to come back late at night. She often pretended that she was asleep rather than have an argument about nothing if he thought she was awake. She often found her face was wet with tears even though she had not realised that she was crying.

The days flowed into weeks, her parent's car had been a right off and the insurance company offered her a cash settlement; the house had sold very quickly and there was nothing left to do except one thing. She went to see Nancy and Davey.

"Come in Alina, I'm just putting the kettle on,"

"Is Davey in?"

"Yes did you want him, he's in the sitting room, go on in and I will bring the tea through."

"I wanted to see both of you actually,"

"Go on through, I'll be there in a minute."

Davey stood up and gave Alina a hug.

"Come and sit here pet, how are you today?"

"I'm OK. I wanted to see you and Nancy together to thank you for everything that you have done for me these past weeks."

"There's no need to thank us," said Nancy catching the conversation as she came through carrying the tea tray.

They sat for a little while drinking their tea and not really saying very much at all.

"Nancy, Davey, there are no words to express my gratitude to you and I will never forget what you have done for me."

"Stop it now," said Davey.

"No please let me say what I have to say. This has been a terrible time for all of us I know, but especially so for me and I know that you are aware that JJ has not been around much to help. Anyway what I am trying to say is there are some things that belonged to Mum and Dad that I want you to have, and I'm sure that they would want that too."

"You've given us enough lass, we don't need anything more." said Davey.

Alina took two boxes out of her bag and gave one to each of them. Davey opened his box and in it was Ronnie's gold watch.

"He wore it all the time Davey. I would like you to have it as a keepsake."

Nancy was opening the box that Alina had given her and when Alina turned to speak to her, Nancy had tears streaming down her face.

"These were so special to Bev, I remember when Ronnie gave them to her, it was their twenty fifth wedding anniversary. She always loved opals, but was really surprised when your father gave her them."

They both looked at the matching necklace, earrings and bracelet.

"Memories" Nancy said, "That's all we have of them now and they're precious. I will treasure these Alina."

"I'm really touched Alina." Davey said, "I miss him more than I can say and I will treasure this and accept it with a humbled heart."

When Alina left their home, she knew that she probably would not see so much of them. Every visit would be a reminder that her parents were no longer next door. There was a feeling of finality to their goodbyes that day. She would come back, but she didn't know when.

She had been operating on autopilot and now there was nothing to occupy her days or sleepless nights. She caught sight of herself in a shop window a few months after the funeral and was shocked to see her reflection. There were dark shadows under her eyes, her face looked gaunt, and her hair looked limp and lifeless. On impulse, she went into a nearby salon and asked to have her hair cropped short. The receptionist told her that she had had a cancellation and advised her that if she could wait ten minutes someone would be available.

An hour later, she came out of the salon; her long dark hair was now just a memory. The stylist wanted to shampoo, condition and style it, but she told her to crop it as short as it would go. The stylist tried to dissuade her, but Alina was determined and after an argument, she got her own way. Cutting her hair did not make her feel any better.

She was still grieving the loss of her parents, JJ was indifferent to her loss, her grief, and as the relationship between them worsened, she blamed herself. He arrived home later that night and Alina was sitting waiting for him.

"Look at the state of you, what have you done to your hair? It's a mess."

Alina looked at him her eyes filled with tears; she shook her head.

"Look there is no point in dragging this out much longer, I have met someone else. You don't take care of yourself and I haven't been able to entertain colleagues for months. I don't know what's become of you and I wonder why I married you in the first place."

Alina's mouth was open in disbelief. He was right, she hadn't been taking care of herself and she was struggling with her loss, but if he had given her some support, things may have been different. She had lost weight, wasn't sleeping well, and had been torturing herself to distraction trying to make things right, and failing at every turn. He did not want her; he was in love with another woman.

Suddenly her hurt turned to rage.

"You are a selfish B. Not once have you offered me any support, sympathy, or tenderness. If it had not been for Davy and Nancy helping me I would never have been able to cope. You have always had somewhere else to be, something more important to attend to and I have let you treat me with indifference for months. Do you remember what you said to me when I told you that my parents had died?"

"What the fuck has that got to do with anything?"

"Don't you dare use that language. You said, 'Oh that's not so good' and then you went for a damn shower."

Back and forward the argument went. Even though he tried to turn her words and blame her, her rage made her stronger. She was standing up to him in a way that she had never done before. For the next hour, they raged at each other. She followed him upstairs and still they raged at each other. She began to feel afraid of him as he realised that he was losing the argument and his attitude became vicious.

He pushed her over and she landed on the bed; while she was down, he grabbed her by the throat choking her with his eyes blazing. She drew up her leg, kneed him as hard as she could between his legs, and as he doubled over in pain, she wriggled free, and ran to the other side of the room.

She grabbed her mobile and said, "Touch me again and your precious career will be over."

He looked at her with such loathing and contempt that she wasn't sure that he was even the same man that she had married. He turned and left the room; she listened as he went downstairs, and then she heard the front door slam shut and his footsteps on the gravel as he made his way to the garage. She looked out of the window as he accelerated out of the driveway.

Chapter 17

She could not bear to stay in the house another moment and she began to regret that her parent's house was already sold. Without thinking of what she was doing, she began to pack an overnight bag. She did not know where she was going, but she certain that she wasn't spending another night in what had been her home.

As she was going through the wardrobe, something made her stop what she was doing. Her instincts were buzzing. She began to go through some of JJ's pockets and found credit card receipts for meals at the same fancy restaurants that he had taken her to when they were dating. There were receipts for flowers, chocolates, and jewellery and none of them had been for her. Now she was frantic, and started pulling open drawers, tossing the contents out onto the floor and searching for clues to his adultery. She gathered all the receipts that she could find and sitting on their bed, she began sorting them into purchase dates. Some of them were more than eight months old. He had been lying all along, blaming her grief as the reason for everything.

She left all the receipts on the bed, and the drawers that she had searched lying open. Before she left the room, she glanced back at the mess she had made and almost grinned; it looked as though there had been a burglary.

She left it as it was and he would know that she had found him out and knew of his lies. With her bag over her shoulder, she left the home where she thought she would raise a family.

She threw her bag in her silver MG sports car and with no real idea of where she was going she drove along Duntocher Road towards Great Western Road and continued through Old Kilpatrick and Bowling. She remembered that the Dumbuck House Hotel was not too far away from where she was. She picked up the Glasgow Road in Dumbarton. As she approached the hotel, she hoped that they would have a vacancy and if they didn't she would just keep driving until she found somewhere to stay.

The hotel was a pretty white two story building that was around two hundred years old, but it was well maintained and had been modernised in keeping with its old world charm. She parked her car in the car park, threw her bag over her shoulder, and tried to look confident in spite of how she felt. The receptionist was polite and friendly and confirmed that they did have a vacancy. As she completed the registration form, she noticed that her room number was eleven; eleven, the number for justice and balance. She took some comfort in that.

The room that she had been given was a large room facing outwards over the front of the hotel. There was a king size bed dressed with white linen sheets, duvet, and pillows, accessorised with a turquoise silk throw and cushions. A matching headboard and curtains gave the room an elegant yet restful appearance.

She unpacked her bag, and began to hang up the few things that she had brought with her. She took her toilet and make up bag through to the bathroom and as she was putting her overnight bag away she realised that she had brought her trinket box.

She opened the small wooden trinket box and scattered the contents on the bed, then sat down to go through the treasures that were there. There was a shell from the beach, which was a reminder of the first picnic that she and JJ had shared. She threw it in the waste paper bin. She picked up the odd pearl earring that had been her mothers and she could remember, as a child, asking her mother if she could keep it. There was a tiny witch on a broomstick that had come from a Christmas cracker, and various ticket stubs from places that she had gone to with JJ. The ticket stubs joined the seashell in the bin. She tenderly handled an old tiepin that had been her fathers and held it sadly in her hand. So many memories, some good, and some not so good flashed back.

Among all the trinkets was a round wooden carving measuring almost two inches across. It looked very old and was worn smooth around the edges and on one side, but beautifully carved on the face of it was a rose. She looked closely at it and admired the details. She thought back and remembered that she had bought it on one of the last shopping trips with her mother. They had gone into several antique and charity shops and she remembered that she had looked at it for a few moments, decided against it and then went back to the counter and bought. She remembered laughing with her mother over the purchase and her Mum saying that it must have called to her.

She threw away everything that reminded her of JJ and sat on the bed holding the little wooden rose, turning it over in her hand and thinking about her future. Her stomach churned with anxiety as she worried about her next step. She went to the side dresser and picked up the kettle to take it to the bathroom to rinse it out. She filled the kettle from a bottle of fresh water that was on the courtesy tray and set the kettle to boil. When the kettle boiled Alina went through the motions of making coffee then kicked off her shoes and sat back on the bed with the little rose just laying there beside her. She picked up the complementary newspaper from the bedside table. She was not really reading it, just turning pages numbly while her head was somewhere else and occasionally staring at the opposite wall. Collecting herself again, she turned another page and a box advert drew her attention.

PSYCHIC ROAD SHOWS

Britain's top Psychics

No appointment necessary

Her heart flipped, the hotel that she was staying in was holding the event the next day.

Alina had her own deck of Tarot cards and had read for friends, but had always kept them out of JJ's sight. He was against 'things like that' and his ridicule of her interests had made her put them away, but she wondered now if by putting them away she was also putting her own essence away too.

When did she stop being herself she wondered? She realized that day by day and bit by bit he had been reshaping her ideas and moulding her into being someone that she was not. She realized that she had no one to blame, but herself because she had allowed this to go on.

Her parents were never sure of her choice of life partner and neither were her friends, but she was caught up in the romance and charm of him and could only see what he wanted her to see. One by one, she had lost touch with friends. He always dissuaded her from them, casting his negative thoughts and feelings on her about her friends until it was easier to live by his opinions.

The next morning, she showered, did the best she could with her cropped hair, and resented the fact that in her angst she had cut it so short. Alina looked through her makeup bag and found some lipstick, blusher, eye shadow, and mascara. Feeling a little more confident, she was about to go downstairs to check out the psychic fare when she glanced at the bedside table and saw the wooden rose. She went over, picked it up, stroked it with her thumb, and put it in her pocket. Before JJ, she had always worn a pouch on cord around her neck and in it she carried little things that held some significance to her. She resolved to start carrying a pouch of special things again. Life was better when she had done that.

Chapter 18

There were several people moving around the reception area as she approached the room where she assumed the psychics were and spoke to a woman who looked as though she was the organiser.

"Excuse me."

"Where have you been, you are late?" the woman said taking her by the arm and leading her into the room. "We have people waiting."

"I am sorry, there has been a misunderstanding," she replied as the woman talked over her.

"I don't need to hear your excuse just now we don't have time, where are your things?"

"I am trying to tell you; I came to make an appointment."

The woman drew back and looked at her deeply. She felt as though she was looking into her soul.

"Let's start again," the woman said, "My name is Madame Cassandra, I apologise for my mistake, but I want to ask you a question and I am sure the answer is going to be yes. Do you read the cards?"

"Well yes, but not for a long time I just came to…"

"I knew it," the woman interrupted "I know a psychic when I see one, even if you do not know it yourself. Help me out dear, a new reader should have arrived last night. You can take her place, sit here and I will make sure that you get plenty of business today."

She gave Alina that piercing look again as she guided her to a table and chair.

"Consider it destiny guiding you," Cassandra said.

"I don't have anything to work with," said Alina in dismay.

"That will not be a problem; I will be back in a minute, now just you compose yourself."

Alina looked around at the other psychics, seated at tables around the edge of the large conference room. A few looked back and nodded or smiled, but Alina was so bewildered by this strange turn of events that she didn't know how to react other than to nod back. A few minutes later Cassandra arrived back with a decorative cloth for the table and a box about the same size as a shoebox.

"I can give you ten minutes to set up and then I will open the doors and let everyone in. We have quite a queue outside now and some have people have appointments so you will be busy."

"Wait," Alina said "I'm supposed to check out; my bags are still in my room."

"Give me your name and room number and I will tell the hotel that you are staying another night," and with that Cassandra just walked away leaving Alina to get on with setting up her table.

She spread the cloth and opened the box to find a pack of Rider Waite Tarot cards, some crystals, a desktop tape recorder, a dozen blank tapes and a notepad and pen. She wondered if this was serendipity or if she was opening Pandora's Box. She wondered too if the little wooden rose was somehow a catalyst steering her in a new direction.

She felt as though the little rose token was calling to her so she put it on her table for luck and as a reminder of the shopping trip with her mother. Within a few minutes, she had her first client, and although she was nervous, it did not show and the client left happy. By the end of the day, she had seen ten clients and had made two hundred and fifty pounds. Cassandra's table fee was fifty pounds from each reader and she covered the cost of advertising and room hire.

Cassandra came over to collect her table fee and have a chat with Alina.

"Well, how was that for you today?"

Alina smiled for the first time in what felt like a while. "Actually once I got started it was ok. I have never read for so many people in one day, it was always a bit of a secret before, I just read for myself or a few friends in time of need."

"Yes, but this is your time of need Alina," Cassandra replied knowingly. "You can join the road show and start a new life or you can go back to misery and confusion, it's up to you, but don't think for too long."

"What would be required if I join?"

"Day after tomorrow we are off to Carlisle, we will spend two days there and then go on to Manchester for two days. After this tour, we take a five-day break and start again. We cover the whole of the UK. The next trip is for twenty-one days and we are off to Ireland."

Alina only took a moment to think, she could go home, pack what she needed including her cards.

"I'm in," she said and felt excitement build in her stomach.

The panic began to build in her chest as she drove back to her house. She made up her mind that if JJ's car was there she wouldn't go in, because she had seen a nasty steak during their argument and she was afraid of him. Her heart was thumping as she drove into her street. Thoughts ran through her mind,

'his car might be in the garage, he might be home and have the lights out.'

Clutching her house keys in her hand Alina unlocked the front door of their home. There was no sign of JJ's car in the driveway and she peeped in the garage window. There was no sign of the car there either and that that reassured her, but she was still afraid that he would return while she was in the house.

She wanted to pack as much as she could and did not want to forget anything or explain what she was about to do. She wanted to be in and out of the house as quickly as possible. She had completely lost her faith and trust in the man that she had loved and believed had loved her.

Before leaving the hotel, Alina had made a list of things that she did not want to leave behind. Going upstairs, she checked her list while her heart fluttered and beads of perspiration began to trickle down her face. She hated to admit to herself that she was afraid of him now, and she was panicking that he would arrive and try to prevent her from going or create a confrontation. She did not want him to make a fool of her and what she was about to do.

She had brought her empty overnight bag with her and she threw it on the bed with two large suitcases from the top of the fitted wardrobes. She noticed that he had picked up all the clothes and things that she had thrown about during her search the night before. She was worried and afraid of how he might react if he came home while she was packing.

She threw as much as she could into the cases, emptied her cosmetics from the bathroom into a vanity case, rammed her hairdryer on the top, and grabbed her laptop in its carry case. She ran into the little study and began to rummage through the desk picking up documents that she thought she should take with her, trying to think of things that she might need, things that he might withhold as a grudge, birth certificate, bank statements, passport, and driving license.

She struggled downstairs with her luggage, in a panic to escape from what had been her home. There were things that she would have to leave behind, but perhaps she could collect them later. Her mind was racing, as she put her cases into the trunk of her car. She ran back into the house for her overnight bag and her laptop. "Oh God," she thought, "My Tarot Cards."

Her mind whirling, she tried to remember where she had last seen them. She would need a cloth for her table. "No," she thought, she could buy one, there would be time to do that when she reached Carlisle.

"Just get the cards," she thought, as she ran into the house and across to the welsh dresser in the dining room. She lifted down a workbox from the top opened it and to her relief, there they were along with Rune cards and a beautiful crystal pendulum.

Back in the car she started the engine, "No!" she yelled to herself, "Leave a note, oh God, paper pen, where?" She couldn't do it; she couldn't go back into the house. He would know that she was gone when he saw the cases and her clothes were missing. Her hands were shaking as she put the key in the ignition of her car and drove away into the night and back to the hotel. She parked her car and the concierge saw her struggling with her luggage and came out to help her.

"Let me help you, madam,"

"Thank you,"

"I thought you were only staying one more night," he said as he smiled at her and competently gathered her cases and put them on a luggage trolley.

"Yes, I am, but I'm going on somewhere else," she replied.

Alina approached the reception as Madam Cassandra appeared from the hotel lounge.

"Back already," she said,

"Yes," Alina replied, "Why do you ask?"

Madam Cassandra laughed,

"You have only been gone about an hour or so, and it looks as though you managed to squeeze a lot into that short time. You look stressed, go up to your room and take a few minutes to freshen up, then meet me in the lounge and we can go over some details."

"I just want to see if I can stay another night and leave for Carlisle from here."

"Leave it to me," Madam Cassandra said, "Off you go and freshen up, and I will see you in ten minutes."

When Alina went back down to the hotel lounge, some of the other readers were sitting with Madam Cassandra. She beckoned Alina over and passed a brandy to her.

"You look as though you need this," she said.

One of the girls smiled at her and patted the seat beside her to welcome her and Alina sat beside her and accepted the drink.

"Sally," the girl whispered, introducing herself. Alina smiled at Sally and then addressed Madame Cassandra. "Thank you Madame Cassandra."

"Just call me Cassandra; you are one of us now."

She breathed a deep sigh as she relaxed into her chair and then she felt the panic begin to rise in her chest as her mind began to race through irrational scenarios.

"What if he happens to come in and sees me here? What if he approaches and starts a scene?"

She could feel her colour rising in her face.

"Could we maybe chat about the details over breakfast?" she asked Cassandra, as she stood up ready to leave the table.

"I would really prefer to go upstairs and sort my things out if you don't mind."

She looked at the other psychics sitting at the table and wondered if they could see everything that she was feeling and all that was happening in her life.

Cassandra smiled, "Off you go, seven am in the breakfast room, I will see you there."

Back in her room Alina sorted through her luggage and checked all her documents to be sure that she had not left anything important behind. She had nothing to worry about as far as financial matters were concerned. The money from the sale of her parent's home, and the insurance settlements were in a savings account in her name only. She was financially secure, but she had only two hundred pounds in her personal account. She had available credit on her personal credit card, but she would not touch the joint savings or current accounts. Then she remembered that she was actually earning money reading tarot cards and smiled to herself.

She did not want anything from JJ, but when they had married, three years previously, her parents had given her ten thousand pounds as a wedding gift. It had added to their joint savings account which had a healthy balance and she knew that she was entitled to her share.

Recognising that JJ had a mean streak gave her cause to think that he would not stop short in making her life miserable even though he was involved with someone else. Although she did not want any part of him, she had taken the most recent bank statements as she felt as though she might need them for any final settlement. She would see a lawyer when she came back from this tour. She hung her clothes, sorted her makeup, and then took a long hot relaxing bath before climbing into bed exhausted.

Chapter 19

The dream woke her; she could hear footsteps walking up and down the corridor outside her room. They got quieter as they receded and then they would grow louder as they returned. She was terrified that JJ had somehow seen her car and was trying to find her. It was several frightening moments before she realized that the footsteps were in fact her heart beating so loudly that it sounded like a person marching up and down the corridor. She could not remember what the dream was about just that there was an old woman in it.

The woman had white wispy hair drawn back tightly away from her face, lined and wrinkled with age. A black crocheted shawl partly covered the old woman's head and shoulders. Below the shawl, the woman wore a thick dark woollen skirt and old black leather boots peeped out from under the hem of the skirt. The hands that clutched the shawl under the old woman's chin looked thin and gnarled with arthritis. Her face looked contorted with grief and she had a pleading look in her eyes. That was all Alina could remember and although the old woman was not threatening, the dream had scared her.

She got up and opened the little fridge in her room, took a miniature brandy bottle out and put the kettle on to boil. She put the brandy in a cup; added a spoonful of sugar, topped it up with hot water from the kettle and climbed back into bed. "I'm just scared," she said to herself, "It's just the unknown." When she had finished her nightcap, she put her cup on the nightstand and got back out of bed to fetch her own Tarot cards.

She was afraid to read her cards for herself, afraid of what she might see. She carefully un-wrapped her cards form the silk cloth; held them reverently in between the palms of her hands and with her heart pounding and her head aching she tried to still her mind and settle her thoughts. She closed her eyes and said a prayer to herself.

Please show me what I need to know when I need to know it.

Help me to listen to my heart with understanding and to speak with wisdom.

Please show me what I need to know now.

She shuffled her cards taking her time to think about recent events and what the future may hold for her, and then she made a decision and said aloud "I am only going to turn one card, please show me what lies ahead?"

She spread the cards in a circle on the bed and carefully selected the one card. For a moment, she held it in her hands, almost afraid to turn it over. Steeling her resolve to what she might see she turned the card over and burst into tears.

As the tears ran down her face, she began to smile and laugh because instead of her worst nightmare she was looking at the best possible outcome, the ten of cups.

"Everything will be alright; in fact, everything will be better than alright."

She closed the cards, folded them in the silk cloth and still holding them she lay down. As soon as her head touched the pillow, she fell fast asleep.

She woke the next morning a six am, put the room kettle on to boil for that first coffee hit and went to the bathroom to take a shower. Fluffy white towels and a basket of delights made her sigh with relief. Shampoo, conditioner, shower gel, and moisturiser, at least she could go through the motions of pampering and lulling herself into believing that all was well.

When she had showered, she came out of the bathroom and caught a glimpse of herself in the full-length mirror that was on the wall. She actually gasped when she saw herself, really saw herself for the first time in, she didn't actually know how long.

Naked, she could see her hipbones sticking out and her stomach looked hollow. She peered up close to the mirror and studied her eyes. Bright blue, they were her best feature underneath her dark hair, but it was not long anymore; it looked as though it had been hacked with a razor. It was too short and there were shadows under her eyes. "Get a grip," she told herself. She had always been proud of her figure and had, by her mother's example, always taken care of her appearance.

Looking at herself now, she realised that since her parents had passed she had forgotten about herself and her self-esteem. For a second, only a second, she thought that it was no wonder that JJ had found someone else and then she remembered his affair had started long before her parent's accident.

"Had it only been the night before last that she had walked out? Blind idiot," she thought of herself.

She felt ashamed when she thought of her parents; she could see her mother's face when she told her that JJ had asked her to marry him. Her mother had put her arms round her and told her that she was happy for her if she was sure that she was making the right decision. In her heart she believed that she was, but she also knew that her mother did not like or trust him. Alina's father never said much about the relationship, but he had a way of observing that said a thousand words.

Alina believed that once they knew him, really knew him, they would come to love him too. JJ had no living family and Alina felt that that was partly the reason that he made excuses not to visit her parents. She felt that he did not know how to interact in family situations. She knew different now, it was just his way of keeping her apart from them and making it uncomfortable for Alina when she went to visit without him.

Looking at her reflection in the mirror, she knew that she had to take better care of herself. She had not worked since her marriage as JJ preferred her to stay at home and since he had a well-paid career in investments, she did not really need to work. She realised this was just another aspect of control, of manipulating her life.

They had entertained his friends and colleagues, but not hers, as he did not really want them to be invited. Dinner parties always had the excuse of networking and her friends were not suitable for that. Before long, she and her friends had drifted apart and she felt guilty that she had neglected them.

"I'm stupid, skinny, and bordering on ugly," she thought "but no more."

She made her coffee and while she was having it, she picked up her mobile phone and switched it on.

It had been off since she checked into the hotel. It was no sooner on than the message beeps began to flood in. Twenty text messages came in, all from JJ, getting progressively more irritated and angry at her "Irresponsible behaviour." "Where are you? How dare you? Get back here right now." Blah-blah-blah, on and on he went, venting his anger.

He did not love her, but he was furious that she would leave. He had lost control of her and was finding that difficult if not impossible to deal with. She sent one text.

"We are finished and you will hear from my lawyer soon."

She would speak to the lawyer who had handled her parent's estate and if he didn't handle divorce cases, she was sure that he would be able to recommend someone who did. From now on she was on her own; she knew in her heart that everything would work out, her cards had confirmed that last night and she would hold on to that thought. Once more, she looked at her five-foot six-inch frame in the mirror. It all begins now she thought to herself.

She took her makeup bag and applied a little makeup to her face trying to disguise the dark circles under her eyes. The hair was another problem, perhaps a spiky do, but she had no mouse or gel. "Improvise... ok," she took some soap that was still a little wet and rubbed it on her hands then used it on her hair as though it was a gel. The effect was excellent.

She rummaged through her clothes and found a simple ankle length black dress with long sleeves and a plain round neck. She picked up a colourful red and black pashmina that had long black fringes around the hem. She had thought would be useful to cover her table. Instead, she draped it over her shoulders and fastened it with a pin. She looked good, shadows under the eyes disguised, a little eye shadow to compliment her eye colour and a vivid red to her lips matching the colour of the pashmina.

On a whim, she unfastened the pashmina and crossing it over and around her waist and fastened so that the long fringes draped down the side. "Hmmm, I look like a gypsy girl," she thought; and that's how she wore it as she went downstairs to meet Cassandra in the breakfast room.

"Good Morning Alina, you look like a different person today, much brighter," Cassandra said.

"Thank you, I feel much brighter."

"I wanted to apologise for the mix-up when you arrived yesterday morning. A new psychic was joining the group and I assumed it was you. I am glad that she did not come now. Destiny intervened."

"I believe you are right," Alina replied.

Over breakfast, Cassandra discussed the schedule for the road show and explained and how it operated. Alina admired Cassandra while she explained things. She looked like a slightly plump, Spanish mama, with sallow skin, a round face, dark eyes and eyebrows, and her jet-black hair drawn tightly into a bun at the back of her head. Alina felt that she could share her fears and worries with Cassandra.

In spite of her gentle appearance, Cassandra was an efficient business woman and her psychic road show was a well organised and successful operation. Cassandra handled all the advertising and advance bookings for the venues and booked the hotel accommodation for the psychics that would attend. There was apparently a bank of about twelve psychics, but they did not all travel with the group at the same time.

Cassandra gave Alina a schedule of the events and the locations. Together they went over the list so that Alina could decide on which events she would attend. "Mark me down for all of them," Alina said.

"Are you sure?" Cassandra replied, "April through to November?"

"Yes mark me down for all of them, there are days in between when we won't be travelling and I can use my mobile phone and email for anything else that I need."

Cassandra reached over the table and placed her hand over Alina's hand. Alina almost drew back, but let her hand remain where it was. Cassandra looked into her eyes. "You don't need to tell me what you have been through, I can read it in your entire being, but you need some stability too and that means you will need an address so that you can have your mail redirected to somewhere to pick up between shows."

Alina bowed her head, the reality of her situation hitting home.

"Look," Cassandra said, "You can use my address for the next few weeks, but then I expect you to get something more permanent sorted out."

"Thank you Cassandra," Alina said. "That's really kind of you, but I think I may be able to use a friend's address."

After breakfast, Alina made a call to Nancy and Davey to explain her situation. They agreed that she could have her mail sent to them and although they were sorry for what she had been through, they were glad that Alina had finally seen JJ for what he was and was beginning a new life.

"Keep in touch pet, we will see you when we see you, and we will call you if anything comes in that looks as though it's important.

Chapter 20

The trip to Ireland had been a success, and she had enjoyed visiting different towns every day even though she didn't manage to do any sightseeing. On her return from Ireland, she checked into the Travel Lodge at Paisley Road Toll. Nancy and Davey wanted her to stay with them, but she needed to stand on her own feet, find herself, and make her own way in life.

She knew she would have to find a furnished flat with immediate entry. Her internet search had shown that there were many flats available, but more often than not, the date of entry would occur when she would already be away on her next trip. She was not yet ready to think about buying a house of her own, and was not even sure where she would settle or when she would want to make that commitment.

Finally, she found one that she thought would be ideal. It was just off Hillington Road South in a quiet cul de sac. It had private parking and a security entrance, two bedrooms with a master en-suite, a lounge, kitchen, & main bathroom. Gas central heating and double-glazing was a plus. It was close to the M8 motorway, which meant that she did not have far to travel to pick up the motorway for her next and subsequent tours with the psychic fair. The best thing about the advert was the words "Available for immediate entry."

She called the agent, a Miss McNeil, and made an appointment to meet her at the property that afternoon. She began to think of what she would need to take with her, "Driving license, passport, and a bank statement should be enough," she thought. How wrong she was. Miss McNeil was very nice and very efficient and the flat was just what she needed. After viewing the flat, Miss McNeil produced an application form and gave it to Alina for completion. She took it with her back to the Travel Lodge and sat down with a cup of coffee to complete it. By the time she had scanned through it, she was disheartened and dismayed. They wanted so much information and confirmation about details in her life and some of them she knew would fail. Apart from that, she did not want any correspondence getting into JJ's hands even in error.

Apart from wanting her contact details they wanted information on where she worked; how long she had been there *'if less than three years, previous information.* her address, and *'if less than three years, previous information.'*

They wanted to know her marital status, if she was an owner, council tenant, private tenant, or living with parents or friends.

"If I was in any of these situations I wouldn't be looking for a furnished apartment," she thought. If all of that wasn't enough the form asked for her credit history, details of her employer and whether she was employed, self employed, on contract, retired or an unemployed student.

She threw the application form to one side, lay back on her bed exasperated and deflated. Lying there quietly she looked around the room. The room was nicely furnished, and it was a good size giving her plenty of room to move around and had everything in it that she needed. There was an en suite bathroom with a bath, and a shower. The double bed was comfortable, and she could relax and watch the wall mounted television set from the armchair that was set off to one side. Ample storage space for her luggage and clothes meant that she would not be tripping over her things and a desk along one wall with an upholstered chair would provide a good workspace. Wi-Fi was free so browsing the internet and emailing would not pose any problems.

She began to calculate her options; staying in a furnished flat would cost her approximately five hundred pounds a month, plus council tax, electricity and gas whether she was in the flat or on tour. If she stayed in the Travel Lodge after every tour, it would cost her forty-nine pounds a night and that meant that five nights would only cost two hundred and forty-five pounds with no additions for electricity, gas or telephone lines for broadband access. Admittedly, that was for a week, but she would be away most of the time and when she was back, it would mostly be for two or three nights. Chances were that her outlay would be less than one hundred and fifty pounds for each period that she was off.

She jumped off the bed and went to the reception area. "Could you tell me if you have any preferential rates for frequent visitors?"

"Yes we have," answered the receptionist, "but only with advance bookings."

"What would that rate be?" Alina asked

"It depends on the amount of visits and how far in advance you book, but if you were coming back four times for example I could reduce the rate to thirty-nine pounds."

"Let me get my tablet, I have all the dates I need in it"

By the time Alina had booked her return dates, she managed to get the rate down to twenty-nine pounds a night and she was delighted.

Alina sorted through her luggage and organised it so that things she would need were in one case and things that she didn't need could be stored in the other case and left in the boot of her car for the time being. She managed to organise her work clothing so that she would just carry one suitcase, her workbox containing her cards, tablecloth and accessories, and her vanity case. Her tablet would give her access to the internet and she could store names and addresses of clients on it. Her laptop would remain in the car with her excess luggage and she could use it if she needed to.

Alina had earned more than she thought was possible during her trip to Ireland. She had taken names and contact details from everyone that had come to her for a reading and planned to contact them in advance of any return trip to ensure a full diary of appointments. She had enjoyed travelling from place to place, meeting lots of different people, and the busy life style.

She began to realise that with each day that passed, she was becoming her old self, and the more she thought about it, she realised that she was more than she had been before. Her previous business mind that was so active during her banking career was now helping her to be the best that she could be following her new esoteric path. She felt as though she could accomplish anything now.

Chapter 21

Alina and Sally, the first girl that she had met when she joined the group, had become good friends and spent a lot of time together. The friendship she had with Sally had helped Alina to find herself again, and although Alina was friendly the other girls that she worked with, Sally was the one that she was closest to.

Sally was the opposite of Alina; she was shorter and very blonde, rather than dark like Alina. She had a serious considerate side to her nature, but more often than not, she was making Alina laugh. Often, at the end of their working day Sally and Alina would get together to have dinner or just chat and enjoy each other's company.

Sally was knowledgeable about many of the esoteric disciplines and had told Alina that she was a white witch. Although Alina followed the pagan path she felt that she didn't know enough to comment.

Sally was nice and to Alina that was the only thing that mattered. She did wonder though if being a white witch gave Sally her calm understanding nature. No matter what happened on any given day, Sally would remain positive and suggest that the Goddess knew what she was doing and that everything happened for the right reasons.

Sally even managed to make sense of the loss of Alina's parents and the breakup of her marriage. She suggested several scenarios that could have happened to her parents, and she explained that witches believe that they come back and experience life and love again. Sally said that when you have a soul mate, you could have that soul mate for eternity not just for that specific life.

Later when Alina thought these things through, she found comfort in realising that her parents would always be together no matter what journey they were making.

As far as the breakup of her marriage with JJ, Sally explained to Alina that she was on the wrong path.

"It's like this," said Sally "imagine that you are walking along a road and it splits in two or three directions. You choose one road and then suddenly come to a brick wall and can't go any further. What do you do?"

"Go back," said Alina.

"Before you go back what do you do?"

"I don't know. You can't do anything else because the wall has stopped you."

"Exactly," said Sally "when you choose the wrong path you are stopped in your tracks and can't move forward."

"Meaning?" questioned Alina.

"OK when you were with JJ who were you and what direction were you moving in?"

Alina sat quietly thinking and then said, "You are right you know, I had stopped being myself and I had become his trophy. I was stopped in my tracks. Even the things that I believed in were pushed to one side, but thinking of it now, I don't know where my tracks are leading me."

"We don't always know where our path leads us Alina, but we should always pay attention to our inner feelings. We should always listen to that inner voice that tries to guide us and tells us when something is not right. When you don't trust your instincts things go wrong, and then things get worse until you stop and change direction."

Sally's words made a lot of sense to Alina and she vowed to pay attention to her instinct in the future. Sally introduced Alina to psychometry; reading an object that belonged to someone by holding it and sensing the vibrations stored in the object. The reader could then accurately tell the owner of the object things that had happened in their life.

They had several amusing evenings practising this discipline and on more than one occasion, they would be falling about on the bed laughing like teenagers.

Alina soon fell into a pattern of travelling with the psychic fair and staying at the Travel Lodge between tours. As always, she carried the little wooden rose with her.

She had started to put little things into the velvet pouch that she wore on a long cord around her neck, and that is where she carried the wooden rose. From time to time, when she wasn't busy, she would open the pouch, take out the rose, and remember the last excursion to the antique shops with her mother.

Nancy and Davey had allowed her to use their address for any official correspondence, and she visited them often between tours and sent them postcards when she was away. They were always happy to see her when she visited during her days off, and she was getting used to the fact that other people now lived in her parent's home. Her life was running smoothly and she was happier than she had been for some time.

The only 'fly in the ointment' was the recurring nightmare of the old woman. She began to keep a notepad by her bed, but as always, when she woke up all she could remember was what the old woman looked like. One night she woke up after having a dream of the old woman, she decided to consult her Tarot cards to try to understand what her dream could be telling her.

She sat up in bed, un-wrapped the cards from their silk cloth, and held them in her hands for a few moments while she pictured the old woman in her mind's eye.

She drew one card, 'The Hermit.'

"Something from the past, a light at the end of the tunnel," she wondered aloud. Perhaps 'the light at the end of the tunnel' was referring to her personal journey. She drew another card and recoiled, anxious; 'The Tower' trauma, disaster, not a nice card to have in a reading and it made her feel concerned. She drew one more card, 'The High Priestess'. Secrets, hidden information. She drew one more, 'The High Priest', information will be revealed - uniforms. She puzzled over these cards not really understanding their significance. All too soon, these things would become clear to Alina and take her on a journey down yet another path.

Anxious about what she had seen and what it may have meant to her life, she shuffled her cards thoroughly and asked into herself what was in store for her, and then she drew one card, 'The Nine of Cups' wishes granted, she thought to herself, closed her cards, and lay down to sleep reassured once more.

Chapter 22

Often during fairs, Cassandra would nominate a psychic to do a demonstration for people waiting to have their cards read, and each psychic had to take their turn. Some readers were accurate in their predictions, but Alina was sure that some just made things up. She disapproved of this and kept well away from those that aroused her suspicions, and Cassandra was no fool either; she soon got rid of anyone that she felt did not come up to her stringent standards.

Alina had performed demonstrations using her Tarot cards, but on this day, Cassandra mistakenly announced that Alina would be demonstrating psychometry. *Was it a mistake or was it by design?* Alina moved to the centre of the floor and stood in front of the eager audience. She asked if anyone would like to give her an object to read. Several people raised their hands, but one young woman was drawing more attention to herself.

"Me, me, me." She was calling and waving her arms to Alina.

Alina pointed to her and the woman, laughing, came forward and handed her a ring before returning to her seat. Alina held the ring in her hands, placed it on the tip of her finger and turned it several times. She closed her hand over the ring and then closed her eyes. There was silence in the room and everyone waited quietly to see what Alina would say. The young woman was looking from side to side grinning.

Alina opened her eyes suddenly and looked straight at the young woman and to others it looked as though she was gazing into the woman's soul. Alina's expression was serious and annoyed.

"You tried to trick me, but you haven't. This does not belong to you."

There were gasps from the audience and the young woman's face was bright red with embarrassment.

Alina walked to the other side of the room where other women sat. She reached over to one of them and handed her the ring.

"I believe this belongs to you."

The woman took the ring sheepishly and apologised.

"I'm really sorry, sometimes my friend is a bit over enthusiastic, but I don't believe she meant any harm."

Alina leaned over and whispered in her ear, "You will have a baby before a year has passed."

At that, the woman burst into tears and her friends huddled round her.

"What did she say?" What did she tell you?" they asked.

What Alina didn't know was that the woman had unsuccessfully undergone fertility treatment.

Alina ignored the disruption, chose someone else to continue her demonstration, and finished to rousing applause from the group.

Later the two women came over to Alina's table; the first apologised for trying to trick her and the second told her about the unsuccessful treatment that she had endured.

"You have given me hope. Thank you very much." She leaned over and hugged Alina.

Later Sally and Alina talked about the experience.

"I knew you could do it, but even I am surprised. How did you know?"

"I don't know, it was just a feeling and at first I was annoyed and then I remembered what you said about everything happening for a reason, so I went with the flow."

Her reputation was growing and more often than not Alina was fully booked before arriving at venues. Sometimes there would be a freelance reporter and photographer waiting to interview her, and she was always a little uncomfortable about that, but Cassandra insisted that it was good for the fair.

One day a young girl about eighteen years old came over and asked if she could have a reading. She was smiling and appeared to be a bright bubbly person. She was wearing a dark coat and her hair was windblown as though she had been waiting outside for a while.

"Of course," Alina replied. She smiled at the girl and gestured to her to sit down. The girl sat down and Alina took her name and asked her for her contact details.

"I'd rather not say, what do you need them for?" said the girl whose name was Alison.

"I drop an email or a card to clients when I am coming back to the area, but it's ok if you don't want to be contacted."

Alina smiled at her and began to prepare the cards for her reading. She shuffled them thoroughly and then handed the deck to Alison.

"Close both your hands and think carefully of your questions, but don't tell me what they are. When you are ready place the cards here on the centre of the mat."

Alison held the cards and thought seriously about her question and after a few minutes, she placed the cards on the mat.

"Cut the deck into three even piles using your left hand."

The girl took her time and made the cuts. Alina lifted a crystal dowser and began to dowse over the first cut, then the second and then the third. In her mind, she was asking the dowser to show her which deck held the answers to Alison's questions. There was no reaction from the first two, but the crystal began to spin over the third cut. Alina picked up the first two and put them to one side before laying the cards from the third cut in a circle for an astrological spread.

She put the cards out by laying the first card face down in the centre of the circle. Moving to the nine o'clock position, she began to lay the cards out, face up, in an anti-clockwise direction. She looked up at Alison who was staring at her intently. Her expression had become worried; her lips pursed together tensely, her brow frowning.

Alina reached over and placed her hand over one of Alison's and said, "You hide your grief very well." and she watched as the tears began to run down the girl's cheeks. Alina had a lump in her throat, almost reduced to tears too.

"Have you ever had your cards read before?" Alison shook her head.

"Do you know anything about Tarot?" Alison shook her head again. She looked terrified. Still holding Alison's hand, Alina said.

"I'm going to tell you a little about myself and I'm going to give you a lesson in Tarot, and when I am finished you will know that everything I have told you is true."

"Some time ago I lost my parents in a tragic car crash, and it was bad enough that I had lost them, but worse was the feeling of terrible guilt that I had let the answering machine take my mother's last call to me rather than picking up the phone and speaking to her. I had been arguing with my husband and didn't want her to hear it in my voice. You know what mothers are like, they always know. Anyway shortly after that my husband left me for someone else."

Alina was watching Alison as she told her story.

"I thought my life was over, and sometimes I even thought of ending it and then something thing happened. I picked up my Tarot cards and I asked one question, I asked the cards to show me what lay ahead and then I drew one card. The card I drew made me cry with relief because it was the best card in the deck. You have that card here." Alina pointed to the ten cups.

Alison's shoulders jerked up and down as she sobbed silently and Alina was not aware that tears were running down her face too. She handed Alison a tissue.

"It gets even better than that Alison, if it had been nine cups I would be telling you that your wishes would be granted, but the ten cups can only be better, beyond your wishes, beyond your expectation."

Alison put both her hands over her face and rubbed at her eyes she was still crying, but now she was laughing too. Alina laughed with her.

Chapter 23

Alina began to explain the Tarot reading to Alison

"Now let's sort out this mess that has been around you. All these dark cards, the swords, these are your problem cards. Each position tells me the area of your life affected by the card whether it's good or bad. I would describe the Tower as your worst nightmare; it's all about loss of control in your life. The Five Pentacles relates to financial matters, look at the picture. That's you in the picture, feeling lost and alone, cold and hungry, feeling as though no one cares.

When I am looking at this second card in the 'house of finances', I look too at the card relating to your career and health because these positions are related. Look at the card what do you see?"

Alison began to describe the card.

"I see a woman behind swords and she is wearing a blindfold and her hands are tied."

"That's you Alison, that's how you feel right now, but remember you have the ten cups and we know that no matter what has gone before everything is going to be better than you can imagine. Look at the number on the card Alison and tell me what it is."

"It's eight." She said.

"The suits only go as far as ten so this means that you have two things to do and only you can know what these two things are. Two responsibilities, two tasks perhaps, but as soon as you have done these two things, the suits have to begin again.

"What number do you think they will begin with?"

"One?"

"Absolutely," said Alina, pointing to the Ace swords in the twelfth house. This is where your anxieties lie and the power of this card will allow you to cut through your anxieties and find a new beginning."

Alison was now beginning to scan the pictures on the cards and beginning to look more enthusiastic.

"Do you see your third house, relating to family and news? Nine Swords, we are getting closer to achieving the ten that we need for the new beginning. You have something to do concerning a member of your family before you can reach that level. The fourth house is showing me your home life, and the Moon tells me about your depression and anxiety."

Alina continued with the interpretation of the cards making sure that Alison understood everything that she was telling her.

"This fifth house tells me about romantic matters and you have an awful card here. The Knight Wands is all about abuse Alison, it can be any kind of abuse, emotional, physical, verbal, financial, spiritual or sexual, but no matter which way it's looked at it is abuse, and you have to get away from it because it or the person who is causing it will not change."

"Your seventh house, which tells me about partnerships and relationships, confirms how this is affecting you. Look at the card and tell me what you see."

"A red heart with three swords piercing it."

"What do you think that means Alison?"

"Heartbreak."

"Yes."

Alina and Alison looked at each other across the table. Alison could hardly believe that Alina, without knowing anything about her, could tell her so much about her life and the things that she was going through.

Alina, of course did not know the specifics, but she could understand the associated events and emotions that the cards were showing her.

"That is the worst of the cards Alison, now let's look to the future for the best is yet to come. This next house deals with endings and new beginnings. Look at the card, look carefully on the Magician's table and tell me what you see."

Alison took the card in her hand and looked closely at it.

"There's a sword there!"

"Yes, there is what else?"

"A branch, a cup, and a coin."

"That's right Alison, although in Tarot we would say a wand for the branch and when there is only one it becomes the Ace of Wands.

On the Magician's table there are four aces, the ace swords, the ace wands, the ace cups, and the ace pentacles, but in your cards there is only one ace missing and that is the ace wands. That ace will bring you new ideas, motivation, excitement and enthusiasm, and it will come within the next six weeks.

In the house of travel and education, you have the ace pentacles, which is fantastic; new doors opening, your chance to learn some new skill perhaps go to college or university. The tenth house is for your hopes and dreams, and you have the ace cups. This will bring you love, joy, and contentment, but you have one problem in the house that deals with your friends and colleagues, and this card 'the devil' tells me that there is a bad influence here and that perhaps it's time to stop listening to someone that is leading you in the wrong direction. It can also mean that you are afraid of someone in that circle. You can cut through your anxieties with the ace swords, which will empower you, and finally the best of all in the middle of your reading the ten cups. It does not matter what has gone before all you need to focus on is your future."

Alison was smiling when Alina looked across at her.

"Thank you so much, I don't know how you did that, but you have made all the difference to me."

"You are very welcome Alison. Are you confident about your future now and what you should be doing?"

Alina stood up and moved around her table and Alison threw her arms around her and hugged her warmly before she left.

Alina took a break before seeing her next client and after having a cup of coffee, she went back to her table to begin again. About an hour and a half later, after she finished reading for another client, Cassandra came over to her table carrying a bouquet of flowers.

"Oh they are lovely, have you got an admirer?" Alina said.

"They're not for me, they're for you."

"What, who from?"

"A girl called Alison, she had two bunches of flowers, one for you and one for her mother. She told me to tell you that she was going home to her mother, and that before she had come to see you her plan was to take her own life."

Alina's eyes were wide and her mouth gaped open at Cassandra's words. She knew that reading cards for people was a massive responsibility and that readers had to know what they were doing, but Alison's message really brought that fact home.

Cassandra put her arms around Alina and held her for a few moments.

"You gave her hope Alina; she only had despair in her life before you read for her."

Chapter 24

Time passed as time does and soon Alina was becoming dissatisfied staying in travel lodges between trips. She had kept some things in storage from her parent's home, and after the divorce, some things from her own home, nevertheless, not having a permanent place of her own to return to meant that she was reluctant to buy things that she saw and admired on her travels. She began to itch for her own place, a place that she could call home. She didn't want to admit that she was also becoming tired of the constant travelling, staying in top hotels while on tour, and eating fancy foods. Sometimes she just fantasised for a plate of homemade mince and tatties or a bowl of chicken soup like her mother used to make for her.

Thinking of that made her think of the last time that she had spent the day shopping with her mother. She fingered the pouch hanging from the cord around her neck. In it was the wooden rose from the antique shop, the odd pearl earring, the mate of the one that her mother had lost years before, her father's tiepin and the little witch on a broomstick. Yet though the memories that these things evoked saddened her, they also brought her some comfort.

She shared her feelings with Sally.

"What do you want to do?" Sally asked.

"I want a home; I want to stop travelling about."

"Are you going to stop seeing clients?"

"No definitely not, I love what I do and I love feeling as though I have helped people to make choices. No I don't what to stop, but I want to be in the one place where people can come and see me in my own place."

"So where do you want to live?"

"Definitely Glasgow, somewhere central, easy access for clients. An extra room to see clients in and it must be somewhere safe just in case JJ gets any stupid ideas."

JJ had continued to harass her even after their divorce, paying her more attention than he had when they were together. She had changed her mobile number, but if she was going to work from home she would have to advertise her services, and if he was still of a mind to bother her, it would only be a matter of time before he found out where she was. Perhaps she was being paranoid, but the content of some of his texts during the initial breakup had scared her.

"Do you want me to do a spell for you?" asked Sally smiling at her.

"No thank you, you and your rituals. I have watched you so often I could do it myself if I wanted to and I've read all your books too." Alina laughed at her.

"Are you going to tell me that you are not just a tiny bit interested?"

Alina looked at Sally and smiled.

"It's not that I am not interested, I'm just not ready; maybe once I get my own place I will feel more like taking it a bit further. I have certainly seen some positive results from watching you, and many of the things that you have explained resonate with my own feelings."

"Have you read your cards on it?"

"Nope."

"Are you going to?"

"I don't know, maybe."

"You will keep in touch won't you." said Sally, her eyes tearing up. "I don't want to lose your friendship."

Alina jumped up from her chair and went across to hug Sally.

"Numpty, you're my best friend, of course we will keep in touch. Remember I have lost friends through neglect before and I don't plan to repeat that mistake. When I get this house you will be helping with the move and the decorating." Both girls hugged and laughed.

Occasionally, Alina would browse the internet or she would pick up a property newssheet, but as always, the next trip got in the way. One day as destiny intended, she was waiting for her next appointment to arrive when she noticed a newspaper left behind by an earlier client. Alina picked it up to browse while she was waiting and she caught sight of an advert that drew her attention.

Property for Sale

4 Riverview Drive, The Waterfront, Glasgow

This is an extremely spacious three bedroom, (1 en-suite), top floor apartment with lounge, dining room, kitchen, and guest bathroom. Attractive views of the River Clyde and residents' parking.

A reception hallway, bright spacious lounge with fireplace, patio doors, and balcony that overlooks the River Clyde. A modern fully fitted kitchen complete with wall and base units, and appliances. Two of the three large bedrooms have fitted wardrobes, and feature shallow balconies. The property has double-glazing, central heating, and is accessed via secure entry. There is ample residential parking on this development on the southerly banks of the River Clyde and there are excellent transport links with nearby access onto the M8 motorway. Offers around £158,000 are invited.

Throughout the day, in between clients, she looked at the advert again. Her instincts told her that this could be the one.

The last three years had been traumatic to begin with and then transitional as she began to rediscover herself and who she really was and wanted to be. At twenty-nine, she felt that she should be in control of her life's path. She was stronger and more confident in herself and she realized that this was the time to make some serious decisions.

She was still sitting at her table with her cards in front of her while she thought about the property at Riverview Drive. She reached out, placed her left hand over her Tarot deck, and then fanned them out in a semi circle. She closed her eyes, touched one card, opened her eyes, and turned the card over.

The card she had was 'The Hanged Man'. This was a good sign indicating life-changing events. The number associated with it was twelve, adding the one and two together would achieve three. Three in numerology meant growth, expansion, and fruitfulness.

She spoke to Sally over dinner that night.

"I read my cards, well one card."

"What! When?" exclaimed Sally

"Today, in between clients, I pulled a card."

"Whatever for?"

"I saw a house advertised that might be the one."

"And you never told me"

"I'm telling you now." Alina laughed.

"Where is it, what's it like, tell me all about it?"

Alina had cut the advert out and had put it in her handbag. She drew it out and handed it over to Sally.

"Wow Alina, this looks great. I love it. What are you planning to do about it?"

This was the last day of what had been a fourteen-day tour and they were at the Concert Hall in Glasgow. She would have five days off and that was plenty of time to arrange a viewing, and if all went well, to see her lawyer before the next tour was due to start.

"Well if you don't have any plans for tomorrow I thought that I would call the agent to arrange a viewing, and I thought my best friend would come with me."

"You just try and hold me back. Oh I'm so excited now."

They chatted over their meal and Alina said she would call Sally to let her know what time to meet her at the flat. Sally left to go to her home in Largs and Alina went back to her usual Travel Lodge. She called the estate agent in the morning and the appointment was set for noon that day. She could feel things falling into place.

Chapter 25

The Country Wide estate agent was waiting for them when they arrived and very professionally showed them around the flat. Alina could see that Sally could hardly contain her excitement. She kept glancing over at Alina behind the agents back and mouthing "Wow." Alina loved the apartment; she stood at the little balcony and looked across the Clyde. She could see the 'Squiggly Bridge', and from the apartment, she could walk over the bridge into the city centre to browse the shops, visit chic bars or restaurants, or she could just walk along to the left from the apartment and she would be at The Quay. There was a cinema and several restaurants there too.

"Maybe I could get a little dog." She wondered.

"Are dogs, pets allowed in these apartments?" she asked the agent.

"Yes absolutely, the walkway outside is ideal for walking a dog and your next door neighbour has a little 'Scotty' dog. She is very friendly."

"The woman or the 'Scotty' dog?" Alina heard Sally saying as she laughed at her own joke.

"Sally!" Alina reprimanded her, but could hardly contain her own laughter.

The estate agent laughed too. "Actually they are both very friendly, Mrs Brodie is my aunt, and Jock's the dog. I'm a dog lover so it would be hard for me not to like Jock."

Sally was still making faces and she raised her eyebrows at Alina as she walked out of the agent's line of sight. She nodded at the estate agent behind his back and mouthed "Nice butt", making a grabbing gesture with both hands as she did so. Alina turned quickly away from Sally. She could not look at her without laughing; she could feel her face blushing.

He did have a nice butt, he was about six foot and lean, but not skinny. He had a look about him that said he enjoyed a game of football or tennis. He looked fit in more ways than one. His dark hair was nicely styled, but had an almost unruly look to it. The agent interrupted her thoughts and she was almost embarrassed as though he knew that she had been thinking of him.

"I will leave you ladies here for a bit to browse around the apartment on your own. Just close the door behind you and I will meet you in the car park."

He offered his hand and as Alina placed her hand in his she said, "Thanks, Mr Buchanan, we won't take too long."

"Please, call me Ronnie," he said, still holding her hand.

"Oh!"

"Something wrong?" he questioned at her exclamation. They were still holding hands and making direct eye contact and as far as Sally was concerned for far too long.

"No, no nothing, that was my father's name, you just surprised me that's all. It's not a name I hear often these days."

Sally was almost dancing behind him mouthing, "It's a sign it's a sign."

Alina ignored her, and smiled at Ronnie releasing her hand from his.

"We will be down stairs shortly."

As he left the apartment, Sally and Alina giggled at each other.

"You are such a bad influence Sally."

"That's why you love me. I make you laugh and I can remember a time when we first met that I wondered if you knew how to laugh." Changing the subject quickly, she added "But he is nice and the apartment is fabulous. What are you going to do?"

"I'm going to make an offer; I want this house, I want it to be my home, it feels right."

"Wait, don't you think you should see if you can get a mortgage first?"

"Actually I don't need a mortgage, I have enough in the bank to just buy it."

"Excuse me, do you mean we have been friends all this time and you never let on that you are loaded? Well I know who is buying lunch," said Sally as she hooked her arm through Alina's arm. "Let's go and have that lunch now."

They went downstairs and met Ronnie in the car park. He handed her the home report.

"I've downloaded it already so I don't really need it thank you. You will hear from my lawyer today so you might want to give your clients a 'heads up', I will be putting in an offer, but they will only have until noon tomorrow to accept or decline, and if they accept it will be a cash purchase so there will be no waiting for mortgage approvals."

Ronnie raised his eyebrows, looked at Alina and said, "That was a quick decision; I must admit I didn't expect that to happen so fast. I will speak to my clients and let them know to expect your offer."

They shook hands with each other and then Ronnie nodded to Sally as he got into his car. Before Alina and Sally reached theirs, he was on his phone calling his client.

Alina sat in her car and called her lawyer. "Offer them the asking price with a close of noon tomorrow. Can you have that couriered over to their lawyer?" Alina gave her lawyer the property details and the contact numbers for the estate agents.

"What now?" asked Sally

"Lunch, I'm buying," laughed Alina, "and then we wait."

At ten o'clock the next morning Alina's mobile phone rang and she jumped up to answer it, wondering if it was the estate agent calling, but when she looked at the display it was Sally.

"Have you heard anything?"

"No it's only ten o'clock; get off the phone, they could be calling right now."

"I can't stand the wait; I have been awake half the night, I'm coming over, I'll be there in less than an hour. If the news is good we'll celebrate and if not, well I'll be your shoulder to cry on."

Sally arrived at the travellers lodge an hour later and Alina already had her jacket on to go out.

"Let's go for brunch, we'll go in your car since it's still warm."

They went to one of the cafe bars in the city and ordered breakfast and coffee. "Make sure you can get a signal in here," said Sally.

"What for?"

"In case the agent or your lawyer calls of course," replied Sally,

"Oh I don't need to bother about that."

"Why! Have you gone off the idea?" said Sally dismayed at Alina and surprised that she had changed her mind.

"No I haven't changed my mind," she said calmly stirring her coffee. She looked up at Sally and grinned. "It's mine, it's mine, my lawyer called right after you, and my offer has been accepted."

"OH MY GOD oh my God, oh my God," said Sally bouncing up and down in her seat. "How could you hold that in?"

Alina laughed, "So that I could see this reaction."

Both girls had tears in their eyes and both were happy with the result.

"You've bought a house; I can't believe it, that was so fast."

"Well the offer has been accepted, but it will be about six weeks before all the paperwork, searches and stuff has been completed, but my lawyer will get the missives signed as soon as possible and my accountant will arrange for the funds to be released."

"What are you going to say to Cassandra? She'll be upset when you tell her you're leaving."

"I'll be upset too and I am dreading her disappointment. She has been so good to me, and if it wasn't for Cassandra, who knows what I would be doing or where I would be right now. She changed my life, and both of you helped me to find myself."

Chapter 26

When Sally dropped Alina back at the Travellers Lodge, Alina called Nancy and Davey.

"Can I pop up this evening?"

"Of course, you don't even need to ask, you know you are always welcome here," said Nancy.

"Yes I know that, but I wanted to be sure that you were both at home, I have some news for you."

"Have you met a nice man?" questioned Nancy smiling and hopeful.

"I'm always meeting nice men, but it got nothing to do with that. It's something special and I'm giving nothing away until I see you. Is seven o'clock ok?"

"No, make it earlier; if you come now you can help me make dinner, it's your favourite, 'Haddock Mornay Pancakes'. I can't wait to see you; we have both missed you very much."

"I've missed you both too."

Later they all sat down to a dinner of smoked haddock. The fish was cooked in a little milk and butter, broken into bite size chunks then covered in a cheese sauce. Alina had helped Nancy to make the pancakes flavoured with a touch of herbs, and then Nancy put a large pancake on each plate, heaped a generous serving of cheesy haddock in the middle, and then folded the pancake over the top. Alina garnished the pancake with grated carrot and added the side salad.

"So what's this news you have Alina?" asked Davey.

Alina reached down into her bag that she had brought to the table and handed the schedule to Davey.

"I thought maybe you and Nancy could come and visit me sometimes and maybe I could make you dinner."

Davy looked at the picture on the front of the schedule and then he handed it to Nancy.

"You've bought this, well I'm proud of you pet well done, this calls for a celebration. Let me open a bottle of wine."

Davey left the table to fetch the wine and Nancy came round the table to hug Alina.

"I'm so happy for you Alina and I'm proud of the way you have handled things these past few years. It looks lovely and I can't wait to see it."

They talked about the house during the meal and then went through to the sitting room to relax with their coffees. Nancy and Davey offered Alina the spare room so that they could relax and enjoy the rest of the evening.

During previous visits, Alina had mentioned to Nancy that she had been having strange dreams, but she had never gone into detail about them. Davey had elected to wash the dishes and while he was in the kitchen, Nancy spoke to Alina.

"Are you sleeping better or are you still having the dreams?"

"No I still have them, it's the same dream all the time, and I have been having it more often recently."

"What is it you are dreaming about, you never said before and I didn't like to ask?"

"I see an old lady, white hair drawn back in a middle shed pleated at either side. She looks very sad and it's as though she's imploring me, but I don't know what she wants. She wears a black shawl and a thick skirt that comes down to her ankles."

"Maybe it connects to your gypsy blood."

"WHAT!"

"I said maybe it connects to your gypsy blood."

"Nancy I don't know what you are talking about. I don't know anything about having gypsy blood."

"I'm sorry pet maybe I shouldn't have said, but your Mum told me that one of her ancestors was a gypsy girl who ran off and married a miller's son and caused such a ruckus in the family at that time. Both sets of parents disowned them. I wonder why she never said. It was all very romantic when she told me. That's probably where you get your gift."

Alina's mouth was hanging open when Davey came through from the kitchen and started topping up their glasses.

"Did you know about Bev's gypsy heritage Davey?"

"Married a miller?" Davey replied.

"Aye that's right, did you know about her family?"

Davey thought for a moment, standing with the wine in his hand. "Aye it comes back to me now, I think, no, am sure she was a gypsy girl and the two families banished them."

"Did your Mum never mention it to you Alina?" asked Nancy.

"You know, when I was little my Mum used to tell me a bedtime story about a gypsy princess who gave up her kingdom and ran off to marry a miller's son. That must have been what she was talking about, but I never thought it was real."

Nancy and Davey were quiet as they watched Alina processing this information.

"That's it, that's why I keep having the dream. Amazing, wow, I'm a gypsy, how exciting is that?" She laughed then held up her glass.

"Cheers," she said still laughing. "How would I find out? There must be travellers somewhere that are relatives of mine. Wow, I don't know what to think or where to start, but I am thrilled to bits. I might have family still alive. Maybe the old woman is a relative? Wow, I hope I dream of her again soon, maybe I can find out what she wants me to do."

Alina didn't dream that night and if she did, she didn't remember. She slept soundly in Nancy and Davey's spare room and the next morning after breakfast, she called Sally to tell her what she had found out.

"What are you going to do about it?" asked Sally.

"Nothing just now, I have too much to think about re the new house and organising things that are in storage, but once I am settled I am going to find out everything that I can. I know my Mum had a load of old papers and documents that I have never looked at, but they are in a case in Nancy's loft for safekeeping. When I'm settled you can help me to go through them if you want."

"You bet," said Sally.

Chapter 27

Eight weeks later Alina stood outside her new home waiting for Sally and the removal vans to arrive. She was a different person now, confident in her five foot six slender frame, her dark hair now healthy and long and a sparkle in her blue eyes. She stood beside her car and looked over the River Clyde and back at her apartment on the top floor. Daffodils bloomed on the well-kept grass verges, which edged the residents parking zone, shrubs and trees provided an area for the birds. She watched a robin pecking around and there was a sense of calmness in the fresh morning air. The robin came really close to her feet and she had an overwhelming urge to speak to it.

"Hello Robin, what do you want little bird, have you come to welcome me to my new home, or are you letting me know that this is your patch?"

Sally drove up and laughed as she said, "Do my eyes deceive me or did I just see you speaking to a bird?"

"Yes you did."

"By the way, Cassandra sends her love," Sally said as they hugged each other.

Alina knew that she would miss working with Cassandra and it had been hard saying goodbye, but that part of her life was over now and this was her new beginning. She was confident that she had chosen well and the fact that her house number was four added to that feeling of confidence as the number four indicated stability and security, exactly what she needed and wanted in her life, stability and security.

Before too long the removal van had arrived bringing her belongings from storage, and she spent the next few hours directing the removal men and telling them where to put her things. Davey and Nancy had come along to help and with Sally there too, the task was so much easier. She had ordered a new three-piece suite and bedroom furniture for her bedroom and the guest room. The spare bedroom would have a small two-seater settee, which she found in an antique shop. She had it professionally re-upholstered in rich red velvet to match her mother's mahogany antique chairs and gate leg table that had been in storage.

Nancy unpacked bed linen and made up beds while Davey worked with a hammer and picture hooks taking instruction from Alina about where to hang her paintings. Sally and Alina hung sheer muslin drapes on the brass curtain rails that were already in place over the patio doors, which opened on to the shallow balconies in the lounge and the master bedroom.

After Nancy and Davey went home about four o'clock, Alina and Sally, who was staying over for a few days, took a walk through each room with an objective eye. They started at the front door as though they were entering the house for the first time. The walls were soft shades of cream or oyster making it easier for Alina to place her things without worrying about clashing colours.

With their backs to the main door, they were looking at a wide hallway that now had a small antique mahogany reception table with bowed legs and a lower shelf. Two soft bucket chairs sat either side, which would allow the next client to sit and wait, and Alina would add fresh flowers to the Chinese vase on the top of the table, and some magazines to the lower shelf. Davey had hung three 'old masters' which continued the antique theme.

A door to the right of the wider part of the hallway opened onto a bedroom, which had a front facing balcony overlooking the Clyde. Alina had decided to use this room for private consultations. She had placed the red velvet covered two-seater settee against the far wall, her mother's antique bureau in the corner and on the opposite wall, her mother's circular mahogany gate leg table, and matching velvet covered chairs. Her workbox containing her Tarot cards and other accessories was already sitting on the table waiting to be unpacked.

"I love the fancy scroll work on the chair frames," said Sally.

"Hmm, me too, I think it looks nice and restful for clients, don't you?"

More paintings were hung in this room and these were scenes of trees and landscapes in soft watercolours. On the far wall stood a music centre so that Alina could play soft background music; and a built in wardrobe doubled as a discreet mini office, storing her laptop, files, and other paraphernalia.

A door to the left of the main door led to the guest bedroom and Nancy had been busy in there making up the bed. New bedding was dressed in soft lavender shades; later Alina would add drapes over the bed using sheer chiffon matched with a silk overthrow. The bedroom furniture in this room had come from her parent's house, and comprised of two cream and gold ornately designed bedside chests and a matching dressing table and stool, upholstered in cream and gold to match the furniture. The style was 'French Chic'. The three paintings here were all of ballerinas in various positions of the dance, and Alina had bought these when she was married. Patio doors overlooked landscaped gardens to the rear of the property.

As the hall narrowed, it led to an ensuite bedroom on the left, which Alina would use, and it too was dressed in soft shades, this time of pearl and cream. The furniture in this room was all built-in and comprised of wall-to-wall wardrobes with sliding mirrored doors, which opened to reveal an abundance of hanging and shelving space with room in the middle, which housed a vanity unit, complete with stool and recessed lighting. Alina planned to accessorise the walls with large prints of red poppies and peony roses.

At the end of the hall to the right was the dining room and here she used her parents antique dining room suite. The table was in a six-seat position, but a recessed pullout allowed it to extend to eight seats. There were two carver chairs and four dining chairs with a matching sideboard, all in rosewood.

Alina had hung small prints of posters depicting 'French Cafes' and had placed two large silver candelabras on the sideboard adding a nice touch.

The Kitchen was a dream of modern technology with stainless steel fittings, cooker, oven, and grill. Concealed white goods and a multitude of storage and work surfaces completed the picture.

The dining room led through to the lounge and in the corner was Alina's favourite purchase, a wraparound Persian blue corner suite with deep soft cushions. A Japanese style coffee table sat in front of the suite and two deep matching armchairs sat opposite. Two tall freestanding shelves echoed the Japanese style that Alina favoured, and she knew that there were several ornaments still packed in boxes that would look perfect on these shelves. Muslin drapes dressed the main widows and moved softly from the air coming from the open patio doors.

Chapter 28

The house was in order and all the boxes that could be unpacked were flattened and ready to go to recycling. There were still some boxes stacked to one side in the lounge.

"What's in these boxes?" asked Sally.

"Books, I am going to need book cases for before I can unpack these, but right now I think I need food more. Are you hungry?"

"Starving," said Sally.

"We could order in, what do you fancy?"

"Chinese would be good, Lemon chicken and fried rice."

Alina switched on her laptop and searched for the nearest takeaway Chinese Restaurant and once she had the number, she called the restaurant and placed the order. About fifteen minutes later her doorbell rang.

"That was quick," said Sally.

"It can't be the delivery; how would they get in through the controlled entry? They have to buzz the house number for access."

Alina went to the main door and looked through the spy hole to see an elderly woman with white hair on the other side of the door. For a moment, the white hair gave her a jolt, but she opened the door.

"Hello dear, you're in then, I'm just back myself I've been away at my friends. I'm Mrs Brodie and this is Jock," she said indicating the Scotty dog at her feet. Jock was looking up at her expectantly.

"I've brought you some shortbread and a wee half bottle of whisky. My nephew Ronnie told me you might be moving in today."

Alina laughed and welcomed her and Jock in and then introduced her to Sally.

She looked around the sitting room.

"Oh my, it looks as though you've been here for months, everything in its place, its lovely dear and I hope you'll be very happy."

"Thank you, would you like to see the rest of the house?"

"No my dear, I just wanted to welcome you. If you need anything you only have to ask."

Shortly after Mrs Brodie and Jock left, the buzzer at the main door sounded the arrival of their meal. Alina pressed the entry button on the control panel and when the delivery driver arrived at the door, she swopped money for the carry out bag of food.

While they were eating, Sally asked Alina about the 'gypsy blood story'.

"I was amazed and delighted when Nancy told me about that. I must have family somewhere and I would love to make contact. I wonder if the old woman I dream about is an ancestor."

"Did Nancy bring the box of documents? We could start there if you like."

Alina went to the built in wardrobe in what was now her designated consultation room cum office and fetched the box of paperwork. She was anxious about opening it fearing that the sight of her parent's death certificate would upset her, but she took comfort from the fact that Sally was there with her, and she always knew how to lighten a mood.

Alina and Sally moved to the dining room and sat side by side at the table. Alina opened the box and right at the top was her parent's death certificate. Below the death certificate was a manila folder and Alina opened it to view the contents. The first thing she saw was her parent's marriage certificate.

"Look there's lots of information on here."

"Sally, I can't do this. I don't even know if I want to do this, not just now anyway."

"Do you trust me?"

"Of course I do."

"Ok, if you are happy to let me copy all the relevant documents, I will take the copies on tour with me and I will research them in the evenings."

"Are you sure?"

"I could really get my teeth into this Alina, of course I am sure, and if I find anything I will let you know."

"Thanks Sally, sometimes I wonder what I would do if I didn't have you for a friend."

Alina and Sally took the papers through to the office and copied the documents and then Alina put the file away on the top shelf.

They spent the rest of the evening chatting and before going to bed having decided to rise early and go shopping for more bookcases or shelving.

After a breakfast of coffee and pancakes drizzled with Maple Syrup Sally said, "Right, let's go shopping for some book cases and maybe new shoes."

They took Sally's Nissan, which had more room than Alina's MG to carry bookcases in, and they spent the rest of the day shopping for bookcases, buying new shoes, and having a pub lunch.

On their return home, the girls built the bookcase and set them out in the hall, master bedroom, and lounge.

All too soon, it was time for Sally to head home to Largs to prepare for the next psychic fair. They said their tearful goodbyes and although Alina was sorry to see her go, at the same time she was glad to have her home to herself.

Over the next few days, more boxes of ornaments and oddments arrived from storage and Alina unpacked them and set things out on shelves and in cupboards. It was quite hard for Alina emotionally because she had not seen many of the things that were unwrapped since she had cleared her parent's home.

Exhausted from unpacking, Alina decided on a long hot bath and then early to bed. She filled the bath with water and some relaxing Himalayan Bath Salts, put some ambient music on to play on her stereo, stepped into her bath, lay back and closed her eyes.

"Coralina! Coralina!" the voice called to her, "Coralina!" Alina looked up as a mist surrounded her, but vaguely, through the mist, she could see the old woman, her hands stretched out in front of her.

"What are you asking me for, what are you trying to tell me?"

"Find her, you're the one."

"Find who?"

Suddenly, Alina woke up, still in the bath, music still playing in the background. She had only been dreaming, but the woman had spoken to her and that had never happened before. Alina felt troubled. She thought that she was probably over tired from moving in and sorting through all the boxes. Memories had been stirred with each opened box making unpacking an emotional journey. She tidied the bathroom, threw her towels in the washing machine, and climbed into bed.

The next morning, she awoke feeling refreshed and well slept, and went through to the kitchen to make her first cup of coffee. She took her coffee through to the sitting room, went over to the patio doors, and opened them.

Nancy had brought her several patio plants in large ceramic pots as a house-warming gift and as she opened the sliding doors, there was the robin hopping about among the leaves of the Acer and the fern. She wondered if it was the same robin that she saw when she was waiting for the removal men arriving.

She got bread from the kitchen and crumbled some to drop around the plant pots and she felt happy about the visit from the robin. Sipping her coffee, she watched as the robin hopped about pecking at her offering and thought about what she would or should be doing next.

After having a shower and pulling on her leggings and a sweater, she went through to her office. She searched the demographics of several newspapers then analysed the advertising costs. Once she had done that, she began to think about and plan her own advertising campaign.

There were brochures and business cards to think about, and she wanted to take plenty of time to avoid making mistakes or missing out relevant information.

She had choices to make, she could take her requirements to a professional printer, or she could do it herself. She decided that she would do it herself; she had all the tools that she required, laptop, printer, scanner, and assorted software. All she really needed was good quality brochure paper and card for the business cards, and she could take her time about picking up these things from a stationery supplier.

It did not take Alina very long to settle into a new routine of seeing clients and studying her subject. She developed a new habit of casting a circle each morning to meditate quietly on her new life, and those things that she hoped to achieve. Sally came to stay overnight between tours, and they would see a movie or go out for dinner, but Alina didn't mention that she been casting circles.

She loved her new home and life was good.

Chapter 29

The old woman continued to appear in her dreams, but since that first time, in March, just after moving in to Riverview Drive, she never spoke to Alina again. Mrs Brodie had become a regular visitor, often bringing homemade scones or a pot of soup and Alina appreciated her kindness. She often mentioned that her nephew Ronnie, the agent who had shown Alina the flat, had asked after her and asked if she was settling in.

It was May now and the days were brighter, warmer, and showing signs of the summer to come. Alina had taken a computer course, learning how to build a website, and she was busy in her office modifying it when she heard her door. She knew that it would be Mrs Brodie because the bell for the main door had not rung. She rose and went to open the door and was surprised to see Ronnie standing there.

"Oh! Sorry, you surprised me for a moment. I thought it was Mrs Brodie, you're Ronnie aren't you?"

He was smiling at her, but it was a shy smile rather than an overconfident one, and for a moment, she heard her mother's voice in her head saying, "Not like that smarmy JJ." The thought surprised her.

He had a covered plate in his hand and Alina guessed that it was something from Mrs Brodie.

"Would you like to come in a moment?"

"Aunt Nessie asked me to bring you some scones."

"I am due to stop for a cuppa, would you like to share a scone and a cuppa?"

"Only if I'm not keeping you back, Aunt Nessie said that you work from home."

"I do, come in?"

She held the door further open and closed the door behind him.

"Shall I put these in the kitchen?"

"Yes," she laughed, "you know the way."

He stopped as he entered the sitting room and Alina almost bumped into him.

"This is lovely; I really like what you have done here."

"Thanks, it's very much to my own taste and style rather than following trends. I'm quite esoteric in my taste."

"I can see that," he said. He walked over to Alina's shelves and began to look at her books and her Japanese and Egyptian style ornaments.

Alina went into the kitchen, switched on the kettle, got out two cups and plates for the scones, and began to fill the coffee machine with water for a fresh pot of coffee.

He came into the kitchen and set the plate on the tray that Alina was preparing.

"Tea or coffee?"

"Coffee would be great thanks."

When Alina had seen Ronnie before he was dressed smartly for business, wearing a shirt and tie, but today he was more casually dressed in denims, tan boots with brown leather cuffs and a chunky brown sweater. Very dark eyes, dark hair, and showing a hint of fashionable stubble, made him very nice to look at, but Alina was not interested in romance; definitely not, but if she was he would be worth a second look.

"Here, let me take that," said Ronnie picking up the tray when Alina had finished making the coffee.

"Take it through to the sitting room please."

They sat on the rich blue sofa with the tray on the coffee table in front of them. Ronnie poured the coffee and Alina watched him. He looked up and smiled at her and she almost blushed.

"What?" he said smiling at her.

"Nothing."

She wondered what was wrong with her. She felt tongue tied; didn't know what to say or what to do with herself.

"You said your Dad's name was Ronnie, what does he think of your new home?"

Alina took a breath, "I lost both my parents a few years ago. My Dad had a heart attack when they went out for the day, and my Mum was killed when their car crashed."

He reached over, covered her hand with his, and looked into her eyes.

"I am so very sorry Alina; I know that pain. A drunk driver killed my parents when I was just fourteen. My mother died immediately, but my father was in a coma for a long time before his body finally gave up the struggle. I went off the rails a bit, got into the wrong company, and missed a lot of school, but Auntie Nessie took charge and I wouldn't be who I am today if it hadn't been for her love and support."

It was an awkward moment, but Auntie Nessie at the door distracted them, and in she came with Jock, who bounced all over Alina and Ronnie.

"Jock, behave yourself, he has no manners at all," she said, but she was proud of the little dog and she knew that neither Alina nor Ronnie was bothered in the slightest.

"I'm off to the shops now Ronnie, but you've got your key to get in haven't you. Why don't you two young things go out on a nice day like this?"

Alina wondered if she was trying to set them up, and she could see by the look that Ronnie was giving his aunt that he had noticed that too, but Nessie just smiled knowingly and off she went.

"I'm sorry about that Alina."

"Don't worry Ronnie, she means well, but just to be clear, and please don't take this the wrong way, I am happy to have you as a friend, but I don't want anything else."

"Don't worry about that Alina, but we may have to pretend to keep Nessie off our backs," he laughed.

They were still laughing when he left, the awkward moment forgotten and a new friendship beginning. He promised to pop in again and Alina agreed that she would look forward to that.

Alina was settling into a comfortable routine. She kept in touch with Cassandra from time to time, and had dinner with Nancy and Davey at their house or hers. Sally was still touring, occasionally visiting on her five-day breaks, and giving her little bits of information about the family tree that she was researching for Alina.

Clients came to see her often and she read for oversees clients on the telephone. She still wore the velvet pouch on a long cord around her neck and often when she was working, without even being aware of it, she would stop to think of what she was going to type on her keyboard, or say to her client, and she would hold the pouch with her right hand identifying each object by feel.

Ronnie came to visit now and again, and they fell into the habit of taking Jock for a walk by the river. Auntie Nessie had instigated this initially and often watched them from her window. In the beginning, they walked side by side, but apart, however before long, they were walking closer, and more recently they would walk arm in arm. Auntie Nessie was a wise woman in her own way.

"That's nice, that's nice, things are moving along nicely," she would say to herself, smiling.

Suddenly Alina realised that Ronnie was an important person in her life. "*How did that happen?*" she thought to herself, then she began to argue with herself about her feelings and even tried to convince herself that it was her imagination. She didn't open the door when Ronnie came across the landing. He thought that perhaps she was in the bath or seeing a client. He went downstairs with Jock and there was a heavy feeling in his chest, but he wasn't sure why.

Alina sent Sally a text.

"Where are you?"

"On tour."

"Yes, but where?"

"Aberdeen."

"In a twin or double?"

"They only had twin why?"

"How long will you be there?"

"Why all the questions? Two more days."

"Still using the Palm Court?"

"Yes."

"Coming across. Will see you later, ok to share?"

"Yes what's wrong?"

"Nothing. C U in a bit."

Then she jumped up, threw some stuff in her overnighter, and went downstairs and into her car. She was already gone when Ronnie came back from his walk with Jock.

Chapter 30

During the long drive to Aberdeen, Alina thought about Ronnie, and in her mind, she went over everything that she knew about him. She knew that he was close to his aunt and visited her often. That showed a caring side to his nature, and although they had spent time chatting while they walked Jock she didn't really know much more about him than that. She knew he was an estate agent and that he lived in a flat in Pollokshaws. She knew the kinds of films and music that he liked, and they had talked about books that they read, but she didn't know anything else about him. He had never talked about anything personal or serious, but then, thinking about it, neither had she.

By two thirty in the afternoon Alina was in the Palm Court Hotel having a late lunch while she waited for Sally. She had already spoken to the receptionist to let her know that she would be sharing the room. Between clients, Sally came out and gave Alina the room key.

"What's wrong?"

"Nothing, does there have to be something wrong?"

"Yeh, there does. Why else would you drop everything and suddenly appear?"

Just at that, Cassandra came over and gave Alina a big welcome hug.

"Oh oh, man trouble," said Cassandra.

Sally turned and looked at Alina.

"Is it?"

"Nooo, I just wanted to do something different."

She gave Sally a look that said drop it. Sally just shrugged and went back to her table and left Cassandra to chat for a few moments with Alina. When they had finished chatting, as Cassandra was moving off, she turned and said, "You know where I am if you need me Alina." She had that knowing expression on her face that Alina had come to love.

Alina went up to Sally's room and lay on the bed to wait until she had seen all her clients. Later they ordered room service and over dinner, Sally risked broaching the subject again.

"Do you want to talk about it?"

"Not really, but it's hardly fair to suddenly land on you and not tell you why, and I don't believe I will get a minute's peace until I do tell you."

"Is it Ronnie?"

"Yes."

"What's wrong?"

"I think I like him?"

Sally began to laugh and Alina was furious.

"I don't know why you're laughing."

"You've always liked him."

"I mean different 'like'."

Sally was still laughing and teasing her now.

"How many kinds of like are there?"

Alina drew herself up and glared at Sally.

"Alright, alright, I promise I won't tease you anymore. Tell me what's wrong."

"I have started getting butterflies in my stomach when I know he is coming or when he arrives unexpectedly."

"Aw' that's lovely."

"No, it's not lovely. I don't want to have these feelings. It will never work, his house my house. I don't want things to change. I'm happy with things as they are or as they were before the butterflies started. I don't want to lose his friendship."

"Did he ask you if he could move in?"

"Don't be ridiculous?"

"Did he ask to marry you?"

"Of course not?"

"What's all the fuss about then?"

"I told you I like him, well more than like him."

"And what is the problem here?"

By this time Alina, her dinner only half eaten, was out of her chair and pacing as well as she could in the small room. Sally was watching bemused and continued to eat.

"I have only known him for six months and look what happened before."

With that, Alina sat on one of the beds and put her head in her hands. Sally sat beside her, drew her hands down from Alina's face and held on to them.

"Alina look at me," Alina looked at her dear friend.

"Ronnie isn't JJ, and you are not the young girl who was infatuated by his empty promises."

Sally put her arms around Alina and told her that the best relationships come from strong friendships. Friends become friends because they like each other and have things in common. Relationships break down because passion rules the attraction, and when the initial passion has burnt out there is only emptiness left.

"Get into to bed Alina, sleep on it and you will see that I am right."

Alina took Sally's advice and slept soundly.

The next morning bright and early, Alina woke up and had a shower before Sally stirred. Alina was filling the kettle for coffee when Sally got out of bed. It was Alina's turn to laugh, Sally's long blonde hair was all over her face, and there were sleep creases where she had been lying on the bracelet that she had forgotten to take off.

"What time do you want to go down for breakfast?" said Alina, still laughing at Sally.

"I ordered room service last night while you were sleeping; two full breakfasts, so that we could chat about the family trees. I want to tell you what I have found so far."

After Sally had showered and dressed, they sat down to breakfast and Sally updated Alina on the results of her search.

"From what Nancy and Davey remember the gypsy line came from your mother's side of the family, so here is what I have found, some of it you might already know, but bear with me. Your line goes back to a Robert Miller.

He was the miller's son that ran away with your great, great, great, great, grandmother. He was definitely sixteen because his birth is registered in 1866 so we can only guess that she was around that age. Oh by the way, you'll never believe what her name was."

"Don't keep me in suspense, tell me."

"Her name was Coralina; I bet that's where your name comes from."

"Never, you are joking, I heard the old woman calling that name."

"You heard her calling Coralina?"

"Yes in a sort of dream or meditation, I'm not quite sure which."

"The more we find out the more amazing this gets."

"You have done some great work Sally."

"I have only just started, there's more. They married in 1882 and had several children, who all died in infancy except their first-born child Emily."

Emily would be your great-great- great, grandmother, and she married Edward Devlin in 1903. They had two children; Paul Devlin was born in 1905 and Cora Devlin was born in 1907. Your great grandmother Cora Devlin married George Alexander in 1930 and had a daughter who would be your grandmother Sarah Alexander. She was born in 1933, and she married Charles McGregor in 1952. Your mother Beverly was born 1954.

Now if we go back to Paul Devlin; he was your great-great uncle, he married a Patricia Cairns in 1933 and then they emigrated to America in 1937, but I haven't caught up with them yet, and really at this time I have no idea where they are, but I will keep searching."

Sally handed the sheet of paper that she had printed the information on to Alina.

"I can't believe that you have found so much information. Thank you Sally. This means that I might find that I have family. Even if they were in America, it would be nice to know that I wasn't the only one.

"Right, I better get downstairs and back to work, I'll see you later then."

"No Sally, I was being stupid yesterday, but as usual you have set me straight. I'm going to head home now."

"Are you sure? You could stay another day."

"Thanks, I'll see Cassandra downstairs and let her know that I am leaving."

Alina was about to speak to Cassandra, but she could see that she was busy chatting to new clients, so they waved and blew kisses to each other.

Chapter 31

Alina had stopped off at the nearest supermarket to get some shopping on her way home, and as she gathered her shopping bags from the boot of her car, Ronnie drove in to the car park and parked beside her.

"Need a hand?"

"Hi Ronnie, yeh, that would be good, thanks?"

"Are you expecting a siege?" he laughed.

"No nothing so dramatic, the freezer is empty, and the cupboards are bare."

Inside she was thinking that she should act normal, but her heart was racing and there were butterflies in her stomach. Why hadn't she noticed how handsome he was, she thought he was attractive, but now he looked as though he had just stepped out of a fashion magazine. He was wearing a chunky dark blue cowl neck sweater over a light blue t-shirt and loose fitting jeans. His face was melting her heart. When he wasn't seeing clients the clean cut look was replaced by a dishevelled casual appearance. She wanted to move nearer him to get closer to that glorious smell of after shave and feel that stubble on her... she stopped where she was; her mouth hanging open, staring at his back as he climbed the stairs ahead of her.

"*Oh my God, what am I thinking?*" For a moment, she imagined his face against hers and she was embarrassed at herself.

He must have felt that she had stopped and he turned to look down at her.

"Alina are you alright?"

"Yes, I just thought of something."

They reached her door and she put the key in, turned the handle, and went straight through to the kitchen. Ronnie followed in behind her and put her bags on the units.

"I'll leave you to it. I'll be next door if you need me." He leaned over and kissed her on her cheek and left.

She stood there stunned; she wondered why he had done that, he never had before. She could hear him whistling as he left and shut the door behind him. She wondered if he was a mind reader, and then she began to think that she had made it happen because she had pictured it too clearly in her mind.

"*I have spent too much time with Sally in her circles,*" she muttered to herself.

"*I'm not a witch. I don't think I am. I just do witchy stuff, hmm… maybe I am a witch.*"

When she shared a room with Sally during tours, she was happy to sit in when Sally cast her circles. She didn't think that made her a witch, but she did have the same beliefs. Sally created magick, Alina only watched. She did believe that God was both male and female, but that didn't make her a witch. She did understand the power of air, fire, water, and earth, but that didn't make her a witch either. She was happy studying her Tarot cards, Rune Stones, Numerology, and Astrology. She was fantasising about Ronnie, but that didn't mean that she was falling in love with him.

"Oh my God, not falling in love with him. Where did that idea come from?"

She realized that she was slamming cupboard doors as she put her shopping away. She dumped things in the freezer without thinking about any kind of order. She began to pace around her apartment. Her energy was throbbing and she did the only thing she knew to settle down.

She had freestanding candleholders in each corner of her sitting room and each held a chunky pillar candle. She looked around her room to make sure that nothing was out of place, and then taking a lighter with her she walked over to the east corner and lit the first candle. Walking around her room clockwise, she lit the east candle, the south candle, the west candle, and then the north candle. She picked up an incense stick and walked around the room fanning the incense into the air.

As she passed her stereo, she pressed the play button to listen to Oliver Shanti, nice relaxing music. She stood in the middle of the room, raised her arms high above her head, and felt energy pouring into her body. Lowering her arms, she sat down on her sofa, leaned back, and relaxed. The music comforted her, and soon her heart was beating normally and her mind had settled.

She closed her eyes and listened to the soft sounds playing in the background. She allowed her mind to wander on a journey of meditation and in the distance, she could see a field, and feel a fresh breeze on her face and in her hair. As she got closer to the field, she could see a small copse of trees. Birds were singing and the sunlight dappled through the leaves and cast shadows ahead of her.

She began to realize that there was an old gypsy wagon hidden in the trees. It had four big wheels and a bow shaped top covered in a dark green canvas. The trim on the wagon looked like oak; the beautifully carved wood was dark with age and the paint had worn through with the weathering, but there were traces of gilt among the patterns. Two long wooden arms stretched out to the front for hitching horses to, to pull the wagon. These long arms too were beautifully carved and painted.

She realised that someone was there. She had never seen anyone in a meditation when she had meditated with Sally, she had seen majestic scenery, wolves, eagles, even dolphins and whales, but this was different. She didn't feel uncomfortable or afraid as she looked closely at the trees where she was sure someone was standing.

The old gypsy woman stepped forward, smiled at her, and handed her a red rose. Close up, she could see the beauty that had been in her face when she was a younger woman, and her hair wasn't white it was silver. Alina smiled in return and accepted the rose. The old woman turned and walked away and Alina watched until she could no longer see her. Then she too turned and walked in the opposite direction through the trees back across the field.

Alina drifted from meditation to sleep and when she woke an hour or so later, she puzzled over the meditation. Rising slowly, she stretched and went through to the kitchen where she had left her mobile, switched it on, and sent a text to Sally.

"Call me when you're clear, xxx."

When her phone rang, she knew it would be Sally.

"Hey what's up?"

"I cast a circle and did a meditation."

"You what?"

"You heard me."

"Well done you, I'm surprised."

"Actually, I have been casting circles and meditating since I first moved in, I just didn't what to make a big deal of it."

"And you never mentioned. Why?"

"I didn't want you to think I was trying to be a witch."

Sally laughed and through her laughter she said, "You don't try to be a witch, you are a witch, or you are not a witch. Being a witch isn't about casting circles. Being a witch is a way of life, being a witch is believing, and behaving in a certain way. Casting circles just helps you to focus on what you believe you can do. I have known you for nearly four years now and in that time we have had many conversations about Mother Earth and the power of the four elements air, fire, water, and earth. I have always believed that you are a witch, but you just didn't know you were, and now you do. What happened anyway?"

"What makes you think something happened?"

"Alina, you didn't call me just to tell me that you had cast a circle, what happened?"

Alina told her about the meditation and the old woman giving her the rose, and asked Sally what she thought that meant.

"She has been appearing in your dreams for how long?"

"Since my parents died, four and a half years now."

"Every time she appeared before she was imploring you, she looked as though she was pleading with you wasn't she?"

"Yeah that's right, always."

"And now she gives you a rose."

"Yes, but what does that mean?"

"Well you must be getting closer to whatever she wants you to do or to find. What's different, has something happened or something changed?"

Alina was silent.

"Something has changed, tell me Alina."

"Ronnie kissed me."

Sally let out a yell and Alina could hear her dancing and laughing over the phone.

"Was it a passionate snog?"

"Stop it! Sally get your head out of the gutter. It was tender; it wasn't even on my lips, it was just different, as though he cared."

"Well I have no doubt that he cares, but in view of our recent conversation regarding your feelings perhaps his are changing too."

"Yes, but did I do that?"

"What do you mean?"

"Did I make that happen, I'm really worried?"

"Did you do a spell?"

"No."

"Well how could you possibly make that happen?"

"I'm too embarrassed to say."

"Alina, tell me."

"When I came home, I met him in the car park and he carried my shopping upstairs. I could smell his after shave and he looked, oh I don't know, he just looked…"

"Gorgeous," laughed Sally, as Alina was tormenting herself.

"Well yes, but I got this overwhelming picture in my head of his face close to mine and his stubble on my skin."

Sally was laughing so hard the tears were running down her face and she was holding her side, which was aching with the strain of her laughter.

"Oh Alina, sometimes you are so innocent, that's not a spell, that's lust. You're lusting after a very handsome man that's been a good friend for the past few months. Relax, you haven't put a spell on him, but cupid's arrow may have struck."

"Do you think that's why my old lady came to me in my meditation and gave me the rose?"

"Could be, or it could be that you are getting closer to something. I don't know, we'll have to wait and see."

"I don't know what to do."

"About what?"

"I don't know what to do about Ronnie and my feelings."

"Alina, do nothing except what comes naturally, and follow the path that destiny lays out ahead of you and you will be fine."

"Why don't you read your cards Alina?"

"You know that terrifies me, I might see something that I don't want to see."

"Then don't look, are you ok now?"

"Yes I am, thanks Sally. I feel really stupid now."

They said their bye's and ended the call.

Chapter 32

Alina went to her office and opened the workbox that she kept her reading accessories in; she drew out the wooden box of Rune Cards and her reading mat and placed them on her reading table. She sat down, unfolded the mat, and opened the box containing the Rune Cards. She sat quietly holding the cards between her hands, she took a deep breath and into herself she asked, "Please show me what I need to know."

She placed the deck on the right side of the mat and deftly using her right hand swept the cards into a circle from right to left. She paused, thought of her life as it was, and then she drew one random card. As always, Alina was afraid to turn the card over, but steeling herself, she turned it over and looked at it.

The symbol was 'Mann'; written it looked like a sharp 'P' with another 'P' in reverse and both letters touching each other. For Alina this was a positive sign, and her experience with this rune indicated that there was someone around her that she could depend on and trust. She wondered was the symbol showing her Sally or Mrs. Brodie or even Nancy and Davey who were still an important part in her life.

As she was thinking about these things, she heard a knock at her door. Thinking it would be Mrs. Brodie, she went to the door and opened it to find Ronnie standing there. His black hair looked dishevelled as though he had been running his hands through it, and he looked stressed when only a little while ago he was whistling as he left after carrying her shopping.

"Ronnie, come in, are you alright?"

"I came to see if you were alright Alina. I was worried that something was wrong."

"Oh Ronnie, I'm sorry if I worried you, it's just, well its just things I can't explain. Come on in and have some coffee. Put the kettle on." She told him.

The Rune Card was referring to Ronnie; he was the person she could trust, why had she doubted that, she already knew she trusted him. It was her feelings that she was unsure of, her own insecurity was suffocating her and preventing her from experiencing her true feelings. She was afraid that if he really knew her and her beliefs, the fact that she enjoyed casting a circle, that she was psychic - if he knew these things, he may just turn his back on her, or worse try to change her, and the thought of that hurt her deeply. She had only just found herself, could she give that up for a man who may not even feel as she did. It would be like JJ all over again, becoming someone she wasn't to please another person.

She was standing in her office staring at the cards on her reading table when Ronnie came through to tell her the coffee was ready. She turned sharply, surprised that he had followed her into her sanctuary and anxious to hide the spread of cards.

"What's wrong Alina, please tell me. I can't sleep for thinking about you since the other day. I know something's wrong and I can't understand why you don't trust me."

"Oh Ronnie," she said as tears filled her eyes, "I'm so afraid that I will lose your friendship."

He drew her towards him, wrapped his strong arms around her, and held her close. He lowered his head and kissed the top of her head buried in his deep chest. The swell of love for her in his heart was unbearable. He just couldn't keep it in.

"You'll never lose me Alina, I'm so in love with you that all I want to do is be with you for the rest of my life. Please don't cry."

She raised her head, her eyes and face wet with tears as she gazed into his deep brown eyes.

"You're in love with me?" she said incredulously.

"I'm in love with you." He smiled down at her.

"That's what has been wrong with me; my feelings for you have been changing and we have spent time together, but you don't really know me, not the real me. There are things that you don't know that you may not like, and I don't really know you either. I'm afraid"

"What's to know that I don't already know? Do you think that I don't know that you are a very gifted psychic, that you see things, that you have your own ghost, that you're probably a witch?"

Alina looked at him, astonished by how much he knew.

"Alina, I have been in and out of your house for more than six months now; I've seen your candles, smelt your incense, looked at your books on the shelves, and heard your music playing. Everything about you says witch to me."

"I don't even know if I'm a witch! And what do you know about a ghost?"

"The old woman with the silver hair who hangs about. I've seen her lots of times."

"You have! Why have you never mentioned her to me and why have you never said anything about the rest of it?"

"Alina I was happy to be in your company, having coffee, taking Jock for a walk, the rest was personal; and I felt if you wanted to share anything with me you would and you didn't, so I respected your privacy."

They were still standing together, Alina had her arms around Ronnie's waist and he had his arms over her shoulders. They had never been this close before.

"Come on let's go and have some coffee."

"Do you want to know what I was doing when you came to the door?"

He glanced over her shoulder and looked at the cards fanned out on the table. "Reading your Runes, Mann, that's a good one to have."

Alina's face was a picture of confusion and surprise.

"You know the Runes?"

"And a lot more besides. Let's go and have that coffee and a long chat and I'll tell you the things about me that you didn't know."

Chapter 33

Alina washed her face before rejoining Ronnie. He had made the coffee and set it on the coffee table in the sitting room. They sat side by side facing each other, occasionally sipping from their cups of coffee, and Ronnie told her his story. He reminded her of a conversation that they had had about his parents dying when he was fourteen. He told her that his life had crumbled before him.

Auntie Nessie had temporarily moved into his family's home to look after him, and night after night he suffered from terrible nightmares. He stopped going to school, got into fights, and then one day he was caught shoplifting. He told her how pathetic it was, because he felt stupid being caught and going through all that for stealing a stupid magazine.

Auntie Nessie spoke to the police and the newsagent and somehow made it all go away. He remembered how ashamed he was and how upset his aunt had been, but she held him close and told him that she loved him, and that she too missed her sister and brother in law, his parents.

He confided in his aunt that his parents often appeared to him and he was afraid of the future. If he had to go and live with his auntie, he might not see his parents again. She promised that she would stay in his home until he was mature enough to decide what he wanted to do.

She told him that if he had no guardian, he would go into foster care, because he was too young to live on his own, but the condition was that he would attend school regularly, get good grades, and stop fighting otherwise he would be on his own.

About nine months after his parents died, he told his aunt that they had stopped coming. She explained to him that they had come because they were worried about him, but now that he had settled down and was attending school, they knew that they didn't have to worry anymore and were able to continue on their journey to the afterlife.

He explained to Alina that this experience raised more questions, and from that point onward, he had read everything that he could lay his hands on about spirits and guardian angels, about religion and beliefs, and that these things had led him to reading about Tarot and methods of prediction.

"We have more in common than you thought Alina; I don't want to change you or anything about you. You are perfect just the way you are. Do you want to tell me about your old lady? I would like to know everything about you."

Alina not only told him about the old woman. She went back to the beginning and told him about her life growing up; about meeting and marrying JJ and how he changed after they were married. She told him that she had changed too, and that she blamed herself for allowing him to manipulate her. She talked about the tragic way she lost her parents and how unsupportive JJ had been. She mentioned Nancy and Davey that he had already met in passing, and how they had been her rock through it all.

They laughed together about how she had joined the psychic fair and how Cassandra had mistaken her for someone else. She remembered the shopping trip that she had with her mother only days before the accident, and while she was talking about the visiting the antique shop, she opened her pouch and took out the wooden rose to let him see it.

"Can I hold it?" he asked.

"Of course."

He held the wooden disc and looked at the delicately carved rose.

"It's a little work of art," he said as he closed his hand over the disc, "It carries some powerful energy, love and joy, sadness and fear, terrible fear and something else that I can't quite out my finger on."

"Yes, I feel that too, I think it goes back to my parent's accident."

"Anguish, that's the feeling that I get, but I think it goes much further back than your parent's accident. Perhaps that's what the old woman is connected to."

"Oh my God, you could be right; and there's more, I think I have gypsy blood. Nancy told me that my Mum had mentioned having gypsy blood, and I then remembered what I thought was a fairy story that she used to tell me at bedtime about a princess who ran off to marry a miller's son."

"You should try to find out about that, my gypsy girl." He laughed.

"Sally has been researching that for me, and she has managed to trace my family to Paul and Patricia Devlin who emigrated to America in 1937. She is going to try to find out more about them."

They talked until the early hours of the morning, and Alina asked Ronnie if he still lived in his parent's house.

"No, when I was about sixteen I began to realise how difficult it was for Aunt Nessie to keep two houses going, so we sold it and I moved in with her. It was selling that house that got me interested in becoming an estate agent, and soon after I started working for the agency, I got the chance to buy a flat. I stayed with Auntie Nessie and decorated it in my spare time and when it was done; I sold it for a profit and bought two more. I live in one flat, but I sold the other and I have been buying and selling houses ever since."

"I have six rented properties just now, but hope to have more in the not too distant future."

They talked and talked until they were both exhausted by the day's developments. Ronnie stood up when he was ready to leave and Alina walked him to the door. He wrapped his arms around her and kissed her tenderly on her lips; her heart flipped a beat and the butterflies in her stomach began a crescendo that rose up to meet her heart. The scent of his after-shave was a pleasure to inhale and his smell, his essence, was all man.

Ronnie savoured her lips, enjoying her taste, he didn't want this moment to end, but he knew that this was not the time to take things any further. Alina had a vulnerability about her and he would not take advantage of her.

As she closed the door behind him, she turned and leant her back against it, her heart pounding, but a smile on her face.

"I'm in love with a wonderful man and he is in love with me."

She heard the engine of his car start and she blessed him with a wish for a safe journey. Auntie Nessie, never a good sleeper, listened to the car driving away and smiled to herself.

"A good match made," she thought to herself, "all that from sending him across to Alina's door with a plate of scones," and smiling, she settled down under the covers to sleep contentedly.

Chapter 34

Alina slept soundly without dreaming and woke up feeling content and refreshed. She cast a circle, and did a morning ritual. When she was finished, she made herself a cup of coffee and settled down on her sofa to compose a text to Sally.

"Ronnie and I talked. Speak later," and pressed send.

Seconds later, her phone beeped for in incoming text from Sally "Good?"

She replied "Great!" and received

"Can't wait, xxx."

Sally called during her next break and Alina told her everything that had happened, especially that Ronnie had said that he loved her. Sally was delighted with this development, as she knew more than most how Alina had avoided any kind of relationship with the opposite sex since her marriage to JJ had ended.

She knew that Alina had a mature, capable nature in most areas of her life, but where men were concerned she was a vulnerable individual. Sally had met Ronnie briefly several times and as well as being very handsome, he appeared to be a genuine person. They made plans for Sally's next visit on her five days off, and they talked briefly about the search for family in America.

Alina went through to her office to check her appointments and to mark Sally's visit on her desktop calendar. She checked and answered emails and from time to time her thoughts returned to the evening before and Ronnie and each time they did, she smiled to herself and enjoyed a feeling of contentment and anticipation.

Still thinking of Ronnie, she began to doodle on her notepad working out the significance of the numbers in his name. She didn't need a graph to work with numerology, but if she had done, she would have written down the numbers one to nine across a page and then the alphabet below those numbers. The letter A would be under the number one and the letter I would be under the number nine, the letter J would begin at one, and so on.

She calculated Ronnie's first name to begin with and discovered that the total was thirty-nine. Adding the three and the nine together gave her twelve and adding the one and the two gave her three. She was happy with that number as it showed a kind caring person confirming what she already thought. Her name number was one and these two numbers added together became four. That was a good combination because the number four gave stability.

Curiosity stimulated she began to work on the vowels, because the vowels gave insight to the inner personality. His inner personality number was twenty, which then became two. Twenty showed her that he considered things deeply before acting, that he was a dark horse and never gave much away. She knew that too, but it was reassuring to have these things confirmed.

It had been some time since she had looked at her own numbers so she thought for a moment and calculated the vowels in her name Alina. With her eyebrows rising in surprise, she realised that the vowels in her name added up to eleven, representing justice, and then two, the same as Ronnie's vowel numbers. More significant was the fact that adding Ronnie's inner personality number with hers gave the number four again.

She was smiling to herself when her phone beeped to alert her to an incoming text. She looked at the display, pleased to see that it was from Ronnie, and read the message.

"Good morning gypsy girl, are you free at any time today? x"

"Clear all day today booked solid Tuesday and Wednesday. Sally coming for a few days Thursday and Friday. Thought the three of us could go and visit Nancy and Davey?"

"Sounds good, I have some news. Good News, C U later. x"

Alina phoned Nancy, and she suggested that Alina join her for lunch.

"I can't come for lunch because I want to be at home this afternoon, but I can drive over now if you are not too busy."

"That would be lovely pet, just you come when you are ready."

Nancy put the kettle on when she saw Alina's car arriving, and they hugged warmly when she went into the house.

"I feel as though I haven't seen you for ages, and I have so much to tell you. How have you been, and where's Davey?"

"He just popped out to get a Danish pastry; he knows how much you enjoy them. We're fine. Take your coat off then come and sit down and tell me your news."

"I'll wait for Davey because he will want to hear this too, but between you and me, there has been another little development."

Nancy was smiling at her and she reached over to place her hand over Alina's hand.

"Oh Nancy, you know you have been like a mother to me since Mum died and sometimes I forget how important you are."

She reached over and kissed Nancy on the cheek.

"You'll have me tearing up girl. We love you too, you're like the child we never had, and we couldn't be any prouder of you if you were our own. So what's the secret you have? Tell me before Davey comes back."

"It's not so much a secret,"

"You've met someone nice?"

"Not met."

"Its Ronnie then, I'm so glad, he is such a lovely chap, always polite."

Alina laughed, "How did you know it was Ronnie?"

"Women's intuition," laughed Nancy, "and I have had a couple of chats with his Auntie Nessie too."

Alina told Nancy about the past couple of days and was just finishing her story when Davey arrived back, armed with a bag of Danish Pastries. He immediately came over and wrapped Alina in his arms, as Nancy went through to the kitchen to bring through the tea tray.

They sat down, and Alina reminded them of the day that they had mentioned to her about the gypsy girl who ran away to marry the millers' son.

She then went on to tell them about Sally's search of her mother's lineage and what she and found so far. Davey and Nancy were surprised and delighted with these new developments.

Before Alina left, she mentioned that Sally was coming for a few days and that they were going to come and visit one evening.

"That will be wonderful Alina. Come for dinner and why don't you bring Ronnie and his Auntie Nessie too if they can make it."

Davey looked at Nancy with a puzzled look on his face, wondering what she was up to and behind Alina's back Nancy winked at Davey, and he just shook his head and muttered under his breath "Women, always up to something."

After Alina left, Nancy told Davey the good news and he was every bit as pleased that Ronnie and Alina were now in a relationship.

"It's about time that she had someone to look out for her." Davey said,

"And he is such a personable young man."

"Better than that…"

"Now, now, Davey, don't speak ill of anyone it's not like you."

"I know, I know, but when I think back to Bev and Ronnie having that accident and everything she went through, and he didn't lift a hand to help or support her."

"It's in the past and best left there," replied Nancy firmly, and Davey went back to his newspaper, the conversation over.

Chapter 35

When Alina arrived home, after her visit to Nancy and Davey's, she changed into smart trousers and a colourful slashed neck top and then added some fresh lipstick. She checked her appearance in the mirror. Like her mother, she always tried to look her best, but she was getting ready for Ronnie to arrive and that made her nervous.

She fussed with her hair, and turned this way and that to see herself from different angles. She grabbed a handful of hair and held it up in a bunch behind her head, she tried it swept to one side, and then she just brushed it down again and left it as it had been. She added a quick spray of La Perla, her favourite perfume, blotted her lipstick. Her stomach was churning in anticipation.

She went over to her candles and lit them one by one, east to north. She lit some incense and pressed play on her CD player. The soundtrack from August Rush was playing and she always found that uplifting and inspiring.

Ronnie kissed her on the lips and held her close when he arrived.

"Hello Gypsy Girl."

"Hello Dark Horse."

"Dark Horse?"

"Yes, I did some numerology on your name today and your inner personality numbers tell me that you are a dark horse." She laughed.

"Did you do your own?"

"I did, I'm a dark horse too."

"You're more of a filly Alina, a gypsy filly."

They were laughing as they walked through to the kitchen and Alina started making coffee as Ronnie got out the cups and went to the fridge for milk. Anyone looking at their ease with each other would have thought that they had been together for a long time.

"What's your news?" she asked as they sat down.

"I've handed in my resignation?"

"Oh I don't know what to say, is that a good thing?"

"I have the rented properties to look after and I have another two that need quite a bit of work. I don't have enough time to work at the agency and look after my properties and fortunately, I have enough in the bank now that I don't need to worry. I prefer working for myself anyway."

"That's great then, I'm happy for you. When do you finish up?"

"Friday will be my last working day; I have annual leave that's been carried over which means my actual leave date is three weeks from now, but Saturday will be the start of the new me."

"What are you doing on Thursday evening?"

"Spending some time with you I hope?"

"You and Auntie Nessie, Sally, and I have been invited over to Nancy and Davey's for dinner. Can you come?"

"I can and I don't think Auntie Nessie has plans for Thursday, but I'll check."

As it turned out Auntie Nessie was free on Thursday, and was delighted to accept the invitation.

Sally arrived as planned and the two young women got ready for their evening out. Sally was eager to hear all about how Alina and Ronnie's relationship was progressing and Alina was happy to share.

"Is he a good kisser then?"

"Sally, enough," laughed Alina.

"Come on no secrets, oh my God you are blushing."

"Stop it you are putting me off; I am trying to put on my mascara."

"Seriously though Alina, I have never seen you this happy, whatever it is that he has done to you its brought out an inner joy."

"Sometimes, when he isn't around, I have these fears that it's not real; and then he arrives and wraps his arms around me and the whole world just stops, and it's only him and me in that moment."

"Aw… that's so lovely, you are making me cry."

As if on queue, Ronnie arrived and Sally got to see their warm embrace for herself as Alina and Ronnie kissed.

"Get a room you two."

Ronnie and Alina both laughed and separated and Ronnie took Sally in his arms and kissed her on her cheek.

"Did you feel left out Sally?" laughed Ronnie,

"Oooh, my knees have gone all week, be still my beating heart," laughed Sally placing the back of her hand on her forehead and pretending to faint.

Auntie Nessie arrived, and together they made their way in Ronnie's car to Nancy and Davey's. They had a thoroughly enjoyable evening and Sally amused everyone with tales of her adventures during her trips with the psychic fair.

Nancy had cooked a lovely meal of Scottish salmon, dressed with hollandaise sauce, and served with new baby potatoes boiled in their skins and drizzled with butter and fresh mint. Auntie Nessie had made meringues with fresh cream and brought them with her as a contribution to the meal, and everyone had these with berries on the side.

Over coffee, Davey, Nancy and Auntie Nessie had a moan about the price of electricity and gas and then reminisced about days gone by dancing at the 'Savoy', although they were quick to add that it was in the later days before it closed its doors.

Alina and Ronnie sat quietly side by side and enjoyed the banter as it went back and forward. The older generation sneaked glances at them and enjoyed watching their closeness. Nancy refused to let anyone help with the clearing up, but Nessie insisted on giving a hand, and the two women went through to the kitchen for a gossip. Nancy asked, "I know you had a hand in this didn't you?"

"Well maybe a little push and a little wish."

The two ladies laughed together.

"I'm glad," said Nancy.

At the end of the night, Nancy and Davey stood at their door and waved everyone off. Davey had his arm over Nancy's shoulder and he looked down at her fondly.

"That was a lovely evening and a lovely meal sweetheart. It's so good to see Alina happy. She has a good friend in Sally and I have a feeling that Ronnie is the one for Alina."

"I think so too Davey."

"Better than that waste of space…"

"Now Davey, let's not spoil the mood by bringing up his name or his memory. Let's leave that in the past where it belongs."

When they arrived back at Riverview Drive, Ronnie kissed Alina tenderly and said good night before going across to Auntie Nessie's having decided to spend the night there.

Alina and Sally decided to have some hot chocolate and they both curled up on the sofa and chatted before going to bed. Alina told Sally of Ronnie's spiritual journey and the fact the he knew about Tarot and Runes, and that he had seen the old woman several times.

"You are joking," said Sally.

"No seriously, he told me he had seen her, in fact he asked me about her before I even mentioned her."

"He is a better fit for you than I imagined, it's good to have a partner in your life who understands your interests."

"I know; I feel quite blessed."

"Do you understand what I am always talking about now Alina? The Goddess knows what she is doing. She led you to that first psychic fair which led you here to meet Ronnie."

"I do now Sally and finally I can look back and be glad that JJ was such a pig otherwise I might never have met you too."

Chapter 36

On Friday morning the girls went out for breakfast to the west end of Glasgow, and then spent a couple of hours going up and down Byres Road browsing the shops before returning to Alina's home to wait for Ronnie who was coming over later. Sally updated Alina on the search for family and was able to tell her what she had found.

"Ok, bear with me, we last spoke about Paul Devlin he died in 1982 and his wife Patricia Devlin died in 1984. Both died in the US. Their son Thomas Devlin was born in 1940, in 1966 he married Jo Beth Mclean and they gave birth to a daughter Joanne the same year.

In 1986, Joanne marries, strangely enough, a John Miller; I feel as though we are going full circle here. Joanne's father, Thomas died in 2009, her mother died in 2012, and we are still in the US. Now I don't know if Joanne and John were just slow about starting a family or if there was a problem, but finally in 1997 they registered the birth of a daughter named Rosemarie.

That makes her eighteen and Joanne and John Miller will be about in their late forties. From what I can gather, so far, tracing your direct line, you have living relatives. Unfortunately, they left America and for the time being, I don't know where they are, but they did come to the UK. I expect they left America because both her parents were dead now."

Alina was thrilled to find this out.

"My goodness that's fantastic news, they could be here in the UK?"

"Yes, they could, unless they have moved again so leave it with me a while longer and I will see what more I can find out. I might be able to trace them."

When Ronnie arrived, Alina and Sally updated him on the latest news and then they began to discuss the continuing appearance of the old woman. Alina had made a list dating back to the first time that she could remember seeing her in her dreams. The three of them went over the list, and all concluded that although Alina had connected the wooden rose as a reminder of the loss of her parents, it was more likely that it was a link in some way to the old woman.

"Have you ever done Psychometry over the rose?" asked Sally.

"No, never."

"Perhaps we should."

"I'm not sure about that, on the brief moment that I held it I could feel a powerful energy, not bad, but very powerful," answered Ronnie.

"I think I should, otherwise we may never get to the bottom of why the old woman keeps appearing."

Finally, after discussing it from every angle, Alina made the decision that she was the obvious choice to do psychometry on the rose.

The three of them stood up at the same time, almost in silent agreement and straightened cushions on the sofa and armchairs, tidied magazines on the coffee table, cleared away the coffee cups and generally made sure that there was nothing out of place or creating an air of disarray.

Without ceremony, Alina lit her four pillar candles and an incense stick. Ronnie and Sally made themselves comfortable on the armchairs on either side of the sofa, and Alina settled on the sofa.

Everyone was quiet for a few moments and then Alina opened her pouch and removed the rose from it. She looked at it for a little while and then, closing her eyes and resting her head against the back of the sofa, she took some deep relaxing breaths. She focused her attention on the rose while she fingered it gently in her hand. Sally and Ronnie were watching her closely and as they watched Alina's face, they could see that she was beginning to smile.

"What do you see Alina?"

"A pretty little girl with dark curly hair; she's about four, and its summer time and she is running towards a little boy who's about eight. He's putting his hand out and she takes it. They are both happy."

"Where are they?"

"I don't know, it's countryside. She's skipping and he's looking down on her."

"Are they brother and sister?" asked Ronnie.

"I don't think so, wait, they're turning, someone's calling to them. She has let go of his hand and she is waving to him. Rosa, her name is Rosa."

Alina opened her eyes and looked at Ronnie and Sally. She was amazed at what she had seen and Sally had goose bumps all down her back. Ronnie got up, went to the kitchen, and came back with a glass of water, which he handed to Alina.

"Drink," he said, "you're as white as a sheet."

"I'm ok, really I am; that was such a lovely picture, I can't believe I saw all that and I could feel it too. I felt as though I was there, right there beside them. Her name is definitely Rosa, I heard her mother calling her."

Sally had not said anything at all and when she did, she surprised Alina.

"I'm really impressed Alina, I knew you had the gift, but I didn't realise how strong it was. I couldn't have done that; I would only have received impressions, but you were right there. You described that as though you were watching a film."

"I know." Alina stretched out the 'know' in amazement. "I want to do it again; I want to find out more."

Ronnie was being protective. "I don't think you should, not just now, take a break first," he suggested.

That suggestion was like showing a red rag to a bull; Alina looked at him, and for a moment, JJ flashed into her head. She read Ronnie's suggestion as telling her what to do and didn't realise that he was concerned for her. He saw the moment in her face, a stubborn set of her lips and eyes that surprised him, but at the same time, he realised what had sparked the reaction.

"I'm not telling you what to do Alina, I'm just a bit worried that too soon might be too much."

She felt like a fool misreading his intention.

"I know Ronnie, I reacted wrongly, I'm sorry I misunderstood, but I think I would like to do it again."

"It's up to you."

Sally observed the interchange between the two of them, at first embarrassed by the static and then uplifted by the love that they showed for each other.

They all took up their original positions and Alina began to concentrate on the rose again.

Once more, she began to smile, "There is a big crowd, and everyone is happy. They are all on the top of a hill and there is a loch below them. Everyone is looking down the hill; it's a wedding, I can see the bride with her father coming up the hill, it's not a bridal dress, but she looks like a bride and she's wearing a veil. The bride is standing at the edge of a heart shape made out of white rocks, they look like crystals." Alina was quiet as she watched and then…

"Wait, it's changing, it's a different time and its cold outside."

"Who do you see?" asked Sally.

"I don't know; it's as though I am looking through someone's eyes, as though I am looking, as though I am that person."

Ronnie was on the edge of his seat; Sally was beginning to feel uncomfortable.

"I'm in an old close and its smelly, really old and dark, I don't like it. I'm knocking on a big dark wood door. Oh, it's ok a man's opening it and I know him, he's laughing. He steps back and invites me in. I feel uncomfortable, I'm in the house it's dirty, there's someone else there, now I'm afraid."

Suddenly, Alina dropped the rose and grabbed her throat. She went rigid; she was choking and struggling on the sofa. Ronnie and Sally both jumped over towards her at the same time. Ronnie was pulling her hands from her throat and shouting.

"Alina, Alina, you're ok, you're safe, I've got, you come back, come back to me. Dear God what's happening to you?"

Sally in a panic ran to the kitchen and ran water over a cloth, then she ran back with it and began to wipe Alina's face with the cold cloth. Ronnie was cradling her in his arms and Alina was sobbing.

"He killed me, he killed me."

"No he didn't you're home, you're safe, you're with me, I've got you babe, I've got you."

Sally went through to the bedroom, grabbed a cover from the bed, and took it back to the sitting room. She wrapped it over Alina who was still cradled in Ronnie's arms. She went over to the stereo, checked what CD was in the stereo, and then pressed play. As ambient music began to play in the background, Alina drifted into a deep sleep in Ronnie's arms. He was almost afraid to let her go, but he gently eased her back on to the sofa, put her feet up, and took off her shoes. He covered her tenderly with the throw from the bed and stood up.

Breathing a deep sigh, he turned to Sally and said.

"What the hell happened there?"

"I don't know Ronnie, I've never seen anything like that, and I had no idea how sensitive she was. For goodness sake, I only taught her to do psychometry. Most people just get an impression, but that was although she was there, in the past, in whatever was going on."

Ronnie was sitting at the table on one of the dining chairs opposite Sally. He was running his hands through his hair as he looked at Sally, his face full of the anguish that he felt.

"I thought she was going to die. I couldn't bear that."

"Don't be silly. She wouldn't have died," said Sally, and she got up and went to the bathroom. She stood with her back against the door and as she slid to the floor, she covered her face with her hands and cried her heart out. At first, Ronnie had thought that Sally was being flippant until he heard her crying, and he realised that she had been as frightened as he was. He let her be for a few minutes and then he heard the water running.

He went to the kitchen and made a pot of tea and as she came out of the bathroom, he called quietly to her.

"In the kitchen Sally."

She came into the kitchen and he walked over to her and put his arms around her.

"I thought we had lost her; I feel so responsible." Sally began to cry again.

"Neither of us could have anticipated that happening."

Chapter 37

Alina was asleep on the sofa when Ronnie and Sally took their tea into the dining room where they could watch her and chat quietly without disturbing her. They were shaken by the effect of the experience on Alina and they were concerned for her. Alina stirred as they talked and they both went quickly to her side. Ronnie knelt down and stroked her forehead.

"Are you feeling alright?"

She stretched and smiled, "Actually I feel good." Then as the visions came back to her, she sat up quickly.

"Oh that was terrible!"

"Don't talk about it just now, you gave us quite a scare, are you certain that you are ok? I'll make you some tea. Ronnie, another cup?"

"Yes please Sally, a splash of whisky in it maybe?"

"In tea?"

"I believe it's good for shock." Sally laughed at him.

When she came back with the tea Alina was sitting up and she had colour back in her face. Sally poured tea for the three of them and then Alina talked over everything that she saw. She closed her eyes and tried to recall every detail.

"I could see a crowd of people, men, women, and children at the top of hill and below I could see a loch. They were all in a happy mood, eager, and looking down a path. Yes, they were standing on either side of a path, and then I could see below them a bride coming up the hill.

I don't know when it was, but it looked like a long time ago. The men were smart, but they looked hardy, as though they worked on the land, and the women were all wearing long skirts and dresses of the period, whenever that was. The bride wasn't wearing a wedding dress as we know them; she was wearing what looked like a cotton dress, it was soft and moving in the breeze and it had tiny flowers all over it. She was wearing a long veil, longer than her dress, that came right down to the ground. I could see wild flowers in the posy that she carried. There were Bluebells and Red Campion and sprigs of Heather with blue ribbons trailing from the posy.

Her father was looking at her, I think she was maybe about five foot four and he looked about six feet tall. He was big in stature, he looked important and he was clearly very proud. She was smiling and nodding to the people who were watching and I could see her glancing up trying to catch sight of the groom, but I didn't see him at all."

She took a deep breath and opened her eyes.

"It was such a lovely scene to see, it was as though I was there."

"Do you think it was Rosa who was getting married?" asked Sally.

"I don't know, it could have been, she looked similar, but older obviously. She did have dark curly hair though."

"What else can you remember?" Sally asked.

Ronnie was quiet, just observing until Sally asked that question. He turned his head and glanced at her. Clearly, he was not sure that he wanted Alina to recall that part of the experience yet.

"Everything changed then and instead of watching a scene unfolding I was part of the scene. I was walking into a dark dingy close. I could smell stale urine and there was dirt on the floor. Rubbish had gathered around the edges against the walls. I felt as though I was carrying something, but I'm not sure what it was.

I was standing in front of a black door and the paint was cracked and peeling. I don't think it was paint, I think it was old varnish. Anyway, a man opened the door, I knew him, but I didn't like him, I don't know why I was there. He was big man he had a rough face and a rough look about him, but he was laughing and joking. He was wearing a striped shirt with no collar and it was creased and stained down the front.

He invited me in, and I don't know why I went in, and I could hear a voice in my head saying, let me get this right, no I can't remember, but it was something about crossing a door. When I went in there was a big fat man sitting by the fire, and the way he looked at me was disgusting, and then I felt the first man's hands on me. They jumped me, I was screaming, but the first man was holding his big fat hands over my mouth and my nose and the other one was groping me."

By this time, Alina was sobbing and Ronnie had moved to the sofa beside her and put his arms around her shoulders to comfort her.

"I couldn't breathe, I was suffocating."

"Shh now shh..." Ronnie reassured her.

Sally asked, "Were you Rosa, was it Rosa being attacked?"

"I don't think so; no I'm sure it wasn't Rosa."

"I don't think we should do any more on this Alina, Sally do you agree?"

"I do. I think we should leave this alone for a bit to give Alina a break from it. This appears to have been building up for some time, since the wooden rose in fact, and there is probably more to find out before we know the underlying cause of this mystery. I have to leave first thing in the morning, Ronnie are you staying here tonight?"

"Sally!" exclaimed Alina.

"Well I will be leaving early and I am not leaving you alone."

Ronnie put his arm around Alina.

"Don't worry babe I won't take advantage of you, not while you are vulnerable, I can sleep on the couch."

"Don't be ridiculous Ronnie. I will be in the spare room; you can be with Alina."

Alina was mortified. It was so typical of Sally to organise her.

"He doesn't have any pyjamas here!" exclaimed Alina and then felt incredibly childish.

Sally gave her an exasperated look that said 'grow up' and Ronnie just grinned.

"I guess that's that settled then," laughed Ronnie as Sally kissed them both on their cheeks and then went off to the bathroom to get ready for bed.

"Would you like some more tea before you go to bed?"

"Yes I would love some."

Ronnie went to the kitchen to make the tea, and when he returned with the two cups of tea they relaxed and chatted about what they would do the next day now that Ronnie was finished with the estate agents. When the tea was finished and Alina could no longer delay the inevitable, she got up to go to the bedroom.

"I will be through shortly Alina."

Later, Ronnie went through to the bedroom. Alina was fast asleep; he sat on the edge of the bed and looked at her sleeping. He loved her so much and he wondered how and when that had happened. He slipped quietly and carefully into bed beside her to avoid disturbing her, and he fell asleep holding her close. Early in the morning, Sally, leaving quietly, woke him up and he was amused to find that Alina's leg was almost pinning him to the bed and her arm was over his body. Rather than react to his natural urge he eased himself out of bed and went through to the guest bathroom for a shower.

Chapter 38

Ronnie was in the kitchen grilling bacon and whisking eggs. He looked as though he was in command of the task of making breakfast. His hair was still damp from his shower and he was just wearing jeans slung low on his hips. Alina looked him up and down from his damp hair to his bare feet and her mouth watered. He was simply delicious to look at. Sensing her presence, he turned and smiled at her.

"Coffee's ready, breakfast will be ready in a minute."

She blushed as he looked at her, she had cleaned her teeth, washed her face, and brushed her hair, but she felt silly standing there in her pyjamas while he cooked breakfast in her kitchen.

"Thanks for staying last night. Where did you sleep?"

"Beside you, you were out like a light when I came through, but you had me trapped under you when I woke up this morning. I saved your modesty and slipped out of bed." He grinned at her and she blushed again.

"Do you want to take the toast through to the dining room?"

She gathered herself and picked up the toast and the coffee pot, and he followed with breakfast on a serving plate and then returned to the kitchen for plates and cutlery.

Over breakfast, he asked her what she would like to do.

"I think I would like to walk on a beach. We could get Jock and go somewhere if you like."

"I'll go next door and get a change of clothes from Auntie Nessie's and I'll pick up Jock too."

"I'm embarrassed; she will think we slept together."

"We did, we slept together all night," he laughed.

"You know what I mean."

"Auntie Nessie is a woman of the world and thinking that we made mad passionate love all night will delight her, so stop worrying your modest head."

When they were both ready they put Jock in the car and drove to Largs. They spent the day there enjoying their time together, chatting, walking Jock along the beach and throwing sticks for him. The streets were bustling with shoppers and day-trippers. About thirty motor bikes were in the car park and the bikers were chatting and admiring each other's bikes. They had lunch at Nardini's then had another walk along the beach with Jock. By the time they returned to Alina's, Jock was tired out, but Alina and Ronnie felt thoroughly refreshed.

"Would you like to go to the Uplawmoor Hotel for dinner tonight?"

"I would love that," she said surprised by the sudden invitation and then she laughed.

"Is this our first date then?"

"Yes I suppose it is."

"Well yes, I would love to go on a date with you." He kissed her on the lips.

"I am going to head back to my flat and change my clothes; I'll pick you up at seven. I'll drop Jock off before I go."

She felt as though she missed him before he was even out of the door.

Sally called during a break to ask how she was feeling after the events the day before. Alina told her that she was none the worse, that Ronnie had made breakfast, and that they had been to the beach with Jock.

"He is taking me to the Uplawmoor Hotel for dinner tonight. I can't believe how nervous I am."

"What's to be nervous about?"

"After dinner."

"Dessert?" laughed Sally.

"Don't be funny."

"Alina, stop over analysing things, what will be will be, and what will happen will happen."

"That's easy for you to say, but I haven't been with anyone since JJ."

"Oh, well then, I think Ronnie has more to worry about than you have."

"Now you're being silly and I'm trying to talk seriously with you."

"Just go out tonight and enjoy it. Ronnie is a decent guy; he is hardly going to force you into doing something that you are not ready for."

"Yes, you're right, I was over analysing. I better go and look out what I'm going to wear."

"Don't forget, matching underwear, preferably sexy," laughed Sally as she was hanging up.

Alina browsed through the hanging rail in her wardrobe; there were a couple of dresses that she had never worn yet, and as she looked through them she decided on a short navy blue fit and flair dress with a slashed cowl neckline. The fitted bodice pinched in at the waist with two deep pleats then flared out over her hips.

She applied a little shadow, some mascara, finished with a quick sweep of blusher to her cheeks, and then went to look in her jewellery box for earrings and a pendant, choosing a delicate chain with a sapphire pendant and matching earrings. A spray of her favourite perfume, La Perla, a touch of lipstick and she was ready. The pouch containing the wooden rose was already in her tan silk clutch bag, which matched the colour of her high heels.

Ronnie arrived on time and when she opened the door, she was thrilled by how handsome he looked.

"You look lovely Alina and smell delicious too." He stooped to kiss her on her lips.

"We're dressed to match," she smiled as she admired him in his Navy silk mohair suit. His navy and white checked shirt was open at the collar, but he had a tie in his pocket just in case.

"I thought we would go for dinner first and then to a late showing of Interstellar with Anne Hathaway and Matthew McConaughey."

"I'd love that; I've seen it advertised."

The drive to the hotel in the village of Uplawmoor took about thirty minutes and they chatted nonstop on the journey. Alina had never been there before, and was delighted to see the small two-storey white and black trimmed hotel as they drove into the almost full car park. As Ronnie negotiated parking his BMW, Alina noticed the Three Gold Star and AA Rosette plaques.

The inside was a delight, with a cocktail bar to the left and a huge brass canopied fireplace in the centre of the lounge. Comfortable sofas and chairs were scattered around the space, and the staff were welcoming and courteous as they showed them to a sofa and offered them drinks.

The head waiter approached and presented them with a menu each, and while they perused a mouth-watering selection of starters, main courses and desserts, their drinks arrived. Ronnie had ordered Alina a glass of Châteauneuf-du-Pape and still water for himself. They both chose the chef's Chicken Liver Parfait with a red onion & orange marmalade for their starters, and while Alina chose the Chicken Lattice stuffed with mushrooms, Ronnie chose a Moroccan Chickpea Tagine.

They talked and laughed while they enjoyed their meals and each other's company. By the time the meal was over neither of them could manage dessert, but they lingered over fresh coffee until it was time for the late showing of Interstellar.

On the drive home, after the film, which they both loved, Alina relaxed listening to Elbow playing on the CD, and she thought over the past months, from meeting Ronnie when he had first shown her the apartment until now. She thought about how they had become good friends and then closer still, and she remembered how he had told her he loved her. They walked upstairs together and Alina unlocked her door and walked into her apartment with Ronnie just behind her. She turned suddenly, stood in front of him, her heart thudding in her chest and said, "This is where I could say, thank you very much, this has been a lovely evening," then she reached up, took hold of his lapels, pulled his face down to hers, kissed him passionately on the lips, and savoured the taste of him. His tongue flicked over hers as he picked her up in his arms and lifted his foot to kick the door shut behind him.

Chapter 39

On Sunday morning, she woke up early feeling content and happy. Ronnie was in a deep sleep as she slipped out of bed and went in to run the shower in the ensuite. She was singing quietly to herself as water ran over her body.

"Meet me tonight by the campfire

Come with me over the hill.

Let us be married tomorrow

Please let me whisper I will."

Ronnie stepped in beside her and squeezing a handful of shampoo on to his hands, he began to lather her long hair,

"What are you singing?"

She luxuriated in the feeling of his hands in her hair,

"I don't know just a tune I can't get out of my head."

"It sounds like the kind of song a gypsy girl or boy would sing."

"Really, so it does, I don't know where that came from."

Later, over breakfast, she could hear the song in her mind. "I'm wondering about that song; do you think it's connected to my old woman?"

"I was already mulling that over."

"What do you think?"

"I think it is,"

"Yes, you are probably right. After breakfast I would like to get out my Runes and maybe ask some questions, see what comes up."

"I think that's a good idea."

Ronnie cleared the table and stacked the dishes in the dishwasher while Alina went to her office to fetch the workbox containing her reading accessories. She set her reading mat on the table and opened the wooden box that contained her Rune cards. She set the Rune box to one side and placed the cards on the reading mat.

"I've seen lots of Rune stones, in fact I have a set of hematite Runes, but I have never seen Rune cards."

"I came across them a few years ago and I find them good to work with when I am seeing clients, I have stones too, but I prefer to use the cards. Do you mind if I light a few candles, set the right energy?"

"I would be surprised if you didn't. Shall I help? You could light east and west and I will light south and north if you like, balance the energy, male and female."

"Perfect, yin and yang."

They stood together side by side and Alina lit the first candle to the east. Together they walked to the south and Ronnie lit the second candle. Alina lit the west candle and Ronnie finished by lighting the north candle. They walked over to the coffee table together and sat side by side on the sofa.

"How are you going to do this?" he asked as he lit an incense stick.

"I think I will just ask to be shown what I need to know regarding the old woman."

She held her cards in her hands, and silently recited her usual prayer finishing with, "*Please show me what I need to know so that I may understand more about the gypsy lady and what she wants from me.*"

She placed the deck of cards on the coffee table to her right and efficiently, using her right hand, she fanned the cards to her left in a semi circle. She closed her eyes, thought for a moment, and then pointed to one. She opened her eyes, drew that card towards herself, and turned it over. She had chosen Eoh.

"This is probably talking about you Ronnie, as this is the card that I often consider to be a helping hand. I have a favourite Rune book on the shelf. We should have a look at what is written for this just in case we miss something."

"Let me get it."

Ronnie came back to the sofa and sat down. Alina fanned through the pages.

"Yes here it is." She handed the book, open at the correct page, to Ronnie as she gathered the cards.

"Traditionally it relates to travel and movement for instance when you are moving home and neighbours or friends gather to give you a helping hand to move to your new home. Since neither of us is moving, it probably relates to you giving me a helping hand."

"When did you last look at this Alina?"

"I don't know, a few years ago, why?"

"There is a sentence here that might be quite relevant," and he read it aloud.

Theirs were travelling folk, but they had settled at this camp for some time.

"And look at the illustration, it's a gypsy wagon."

"Oh, perhaps it's relating to the old woman's background, her heritage."

"Try another; be more specific with your question."

Alina sat with the cards for a moment and asked into herself

"What am I looking for?"

She fanned the cards as before, paused, then pointed to a card and drew it towards herself before turning it over. She had drawn Thurizas, the Rune of caution.

"Look at the picture Alina, it has a rose in it."

"I remember this one; the story tells us to mind the thorns when picking roses, to handle things with care."

"What do you carry in your pouch Alina?"

"Oh my goodness, I didn't make the connection, it's a rose. That's not making sense, I can't be looking for a rose, and I already have a rose."

"It must be connected to the rose Alina, perhaps the rose belongs to Rosa that appeared when you did psychometry. Ask another question."

"This has to be the last one today. I never like to draw more than three for myself."

She fanned the cards, paused, then pointed to a card and drew it towards herself. This time she turned over Lagu.

"What did you ask, Alina?"

"If I am looking for a person, where is she or he?"

"Lagu is caution again; it deals with the emotions telling us to be patient and to wait for the right time before acting. It's not making sense to me."

Suddenly the hairs stood out on the back of her neck, she looked at Ronnie.

"What is it, what's wrong?"

"Whoever we are looking for is in the water. The illustration shows water. I'm sure that we are looking for someone who is lost or hidden in water."

They both jumped up as the patio doors slammed open, blowing out the candles and for just a second Alina saw the old woman.

They stood looking at each other.

"Did you see her Ronnie?"

"Yes, I did, I think we are getting closer. I think it is a woman who is missing and I think she is in water, and it might be Rosa."

Alina stood up, went over to close the doors and as she reached the patio doors she called to Ronnie, "She's on the sidewalk by the river. Oh my God! Ronnie, I think whoever she is looking for is in the Clyde. Oh dear God, it's too terrible to imagine."

Ronnie put his arms around Alina and comforted her as she sobbed.

"We're getting closer Alina, we'll get to the bottom of this, we'll do everything we can to find her."

Suddenly the scent of roses filled the air, Ronnie and Alina looked at each other and smiled.

"Can you smell them Alina?"

"Yes, it's beautiful. It feels as though she is telling us that she is happy with what we have found so far. How are we ever going to find whoever it is who is missing?"

"I think for the time being we need to take a break from this to gather our thoughts, and then we should do some research on the internet and maybe the Mitchell Library. We should be able to track newspapers that were topical during..., oh we can't search newspapers, and we have no idea what period we are researching."

Ronnie looked despondent as he realised the enormity of the task.

Chapter 40

They pondered over the enormity of their task and then Alina suddenly announced.

"I know a way that we could maybe narrow it down."

"How?"

Alina was grinning as she opened her workbox and drew out a six-inch long crystal dowser, which was about an inch thick. It had a copper band over the top with an eyelet, and a heavy silver chain was threaded though the eyelet. Beaten copper spiralled from the top to the bottom of the crystal, with copper wire following the path of the beaten copper. The wire secured two small magnets attached to either side of the crystal.

From the bottom of the workbox, Alina drew out a notepad and two pens, and began to peel off sheets of paper and tear them into small squares.

"I'm intrigued," said Ronnie as he watched her.

"It's my dowser. So what do we know so far?"

"Well we think we are looking for a girl called Rose who was murdered and she lived in a gypsy caravan."

"But we don't know when."

"No."

"So if we guess at when travellers lived in gypsy caravans, what would be your 'guestimate'?"

"I suppose from the 1900's to maybe the 1970's."

"That's good enough to start with," said Alina, and she began to write the years from 1900 to 1970 on eight squares of paper and then lay them out face down on her reading mat. She spread them about, mixing them up and then asked Ronnie to place them so that they were not touching each other. When he had done so Alina placed her elbow on the tabletop to keep her arm steady, and then she suspended her dowser holding the chain draped over her index finger and held in place by her thumb.

She held the dowser over the first piece of paper; nothing happened, then the second and the third with the same negative reaction. When the dowser reached the fourth piece of paper, it began to pull to the right.

"Can you see that?" Alina asked.

"What's it doing?"

"I think it's the fifth and coincidentally the number five relates to questions being answered?"

She suspended the dowser over the fifth piece of paper and it spun fast.

Ronnie turned over the piece of paper and read out the year.

"It's the 1920's."

Alina tore ten strips of paper and wrote each year from 1920 to 1929 on each piece. Ronnie scattered them around the table as before and Alina began to douse once more. There was no response from the douser as it passed over the first six pieces of paper and then on the seventh it began to spin.

"I bet its 1923."

"Why do you say that?"

"A hunch."

"Spill, what gives you the hunch?"

"The number twenty-three is often associated with abuse, turn it over."

Ronnie slowly turned over the paper and jumped back laughing, but in awe of what he saw. The year 1923 was on the paper.

"Alina," he laughed, "you are really scary. Did you even have to dowse?"

"Well yes, I would never have taken the chance on something so important, but I had a feeling."

"Ok what now? We have the year, so that leaves three hundred and sixty four days of newspapers to search through."

"Well let's try adding months such as January 1923, then February 1923 and so on."

They shared the task between them and once more, they wrote the year and month on squares of paper and placed them on the reading mat. Alina began to dowse again but this time the year and months were visible. She began with January 1923. When she reached May 1923, the crystal began to rotate.

"That's it then, it looks as though whatever happened occurred in May 1923, only thirty-one days of newspapers to read, fifteen days each if we do it together."

"We'll go to the Mitchell Library tomorrow if you like." said Ronnie.

"Thanks Ronnie, I'm glad that you are helping me with this."

Monday and Tuesday were clear for Alina, as she had no clients expected until Wednesday, giving her spare time to devote to the search, and now that Ronnie was finished at the estate agency, he could spare as much time as necessary. Since the library was twenty minutes away from her apartment, they decided to walk rather than take a car and have to think about parking in the city.

They admired the library as they approached it and looked at the stunning building with its distinctive copper dome, bronze statue and striking classic facade. Inside was every bit as imposing and whilst it was tempting to spend time exploring various exhibits and collections, they made their way to the fifth floor where archives where stored.

The librarian directed them to back issues, suggested the Glasgow Herald as a good place to start their search, and instructed them in the use of the microfilm machines. They settled down to the task and worked until almost one o'clock. Ronnie turned and looked at Alina who was engrossed in her task.

"How does lunch sound?" At first, she was so engrossed in her study of the material that she didn't even hear him and then she stopped and looked at him.

"Did I hear the word lunch?" she grinned, and they both stood at the same time.

"Let's go down to the ground floor, I am sure there is a cafe there."

In contrast to the main building, the cafe was light, modern, and almost full in spite of being a Monday. They managed to find a free table, looked over the menus and then Ronnie joined the queue to order Cajun Chicken Panini's and coffees.

Over lunch, they discussed their searches. Ronnie had started at the end of the year 1923 on the first day of May, whilst Alina had started at the last day and was working backwards.

"How are you getting on Alina?"

"My eyes are melting," she laughed.

"Yeah, mine too. Have you any hunches?"

"Yes, but I'm not telling."

"Come on, share."

"I'll write it down and we'll see if I'm right." She took out her mobile, opened the 'memo' app, and typed in the date she thought would shed a result, saved the note, and closed her phone.

They both laughed as they gathered their plates and piled them on their tray, before going back to the fifth floor to resume their search. The search appeared to be easier in the afternoon, perhaps because they had refuelled, or maybe they were just getting used to searching. At four o'clock Alina made an announcement.

"Found something."

Ronnie went to join her at her station and stooped over her shoulder to read what she had found. There, in black and white at the bottom of the page were the words, *"Police rushed to the area of Kinning Park to break up an unruly crowd of travellers who were causing a nuisance and creating fear and alarm by tramping through closes, banging on doors allegedly in search of a missing girl. No arrests were made and the unruly mob was disbanded."*

"That's it, don't you think?"

"I think so, maybe," replied Alina.

"Scroll up, what is the date?"

She did as he asked and at the top of the page they both read aloud together,

"The Glasgow Herald Saturday May 23rd 1923."

"What did you think it would be?"

She took out her mobile opened the note that she said and handed it to Ronnie so that he could read it for himself. He looked at the text display and there was the date twenty-third of May 1923.

"Alina, that's just not possible, but I am looking at it. I can hardly believe my eyes, how on earth did you know?"

"I told you, twenty-three, it's a funny number, there are hundreds of statistics about the number; on very few occasions, during a reading, I have known it to represent a soul mate, but I would say that ninety percent of the time, for me anyway, it represents abuse of some form or another."

"Let's go home."

They closed things down, thanked the librarian, and began the short walk home. They were both quiet on the journey and Alina was worried that Ronnie was perhaps having second thoughts about being involved with someone like her. She was beginning to wish she had held her gift back, and then she remembered her promise to herself after her relationship with JJ.

This is who she was. Things that she felt, saw, or understood were things that made her who she was and she was not going to change for anyone no matter how painful it would be.

"Are you angry Ronnie?"

"Angry? What about?"

"About things I see and know."

He stopped there in the street, traffic thickly congested only feet from them, and he put his hands on her shoulders and looked into her eyes.

"Nothing you do or see or say makes me angry Alina, confused, yes, I'll admit to that, but angry? Absolutely not. I admire your gift, but it scares me a little, you are so on point. It doesn't scare me that much though that it would change my feelings for you, if that's what you mean."

Alina breathed a sigh of relief as he leaned down and kissed her passionately on the lips to the accompaniment of passing cars honking their horns. They laughed together and continued toward Alina's apartment. Auntie Nessie joined them for dinner that evening and after she left, Ronnie left to spend the night at his own flat.

Chapter 41

Ronnie had business to attend to the following day and wanted an early start; he also wanted to give Alina some time to herself so that she could prepare to see her clients the next day. Sally was due to arrive on Thursday around lunchtime with the latest news on her search of the family tree, so they arranged to meet again on Thursday to discuss what they had found out and decide on the next step.

Ronnie arrived first on the Thursday and Alina was happy to see him, she had missed his company even though it had only been for one day. He wrapped her in his arms and kissed her on her lips.

"Hello my Gypsy Girl, I have missed you."

"Hello my Dark Horse," she laughed.

"What, didn't you miss me?"

"I did, but I didn't want to admit it."

"Is Sally here yet?"

"No, but I expect her anytime now."

Alina had set the table so that they could have lunch; she had prepared some potato salad, cooked ham and chicken, salad greens, tomatoes and fresh crusty bread that she had shopped for in the morning.

Sally arrived a few minutes later and as usual was bursting with energy and enthusiasm. She hugged and kissed both of them and hung her jacket in the hall.

"Ooh lunch, I'm starved and I have a lot to tell you."

Over lunch, Sally started the conversation, giving Alina news of the last trip and passing on regards to Alina from Cassandra and the other psychics.

"Saving the best till last I have found more family connections."

"That's great Sally," said Alina enthusiastically.

"The last time we spoke about this I mentioned that I had got as far as Paul Devlin who married a Patricia Cairns and then moved to the United States in 1937. In this most recent search, I have found their son, Thomas Devlin. He married Jobeth McLean in 1966 and they had a daughter Joanne in 1997."

Sally stopped to chew a mouthful of chicken and crusty bread.

"Sally that's amazing, I can't believe how good you are at this stuff."

"Wait, there's more, we know that in 1882 Coralina ran off and married the miller's son Robert Miller, and then one hundred odd years later in 1986 Joanne married John Miller.

"1986, that's not that long ago Alina, you could still have traceable relatives," Ronnie said.

"I know; I am excited at the thought."

"Ok, so Joanne and John had a daughter Rosemarie in 1997, that means she'll be eighteen now. I honestly don't know what the relationship will be, cousins I suppose three or four times removed, but that doesn't really matter, what matters is, they are family. The thing is I'm still searching The National Archives, and hopefully I will find something. There is also the 'Voters Roll', I'll search there too, but I am sure that they are here and I will find them."

Alina jumped up from the table and went around it to hug Sally who was sitting on the other side.

"Oh my God that's amazing Sally. I don't know what to think. Goodness! I may have passed them in the street and not known."

"See, I knew you would get carried away with it all, they could be in Brighton or Wales or Ireland for all I know, but I will keep trying to find them."

Alina frowned, but only for a moment and then she was excited again.

"I still think the progress you have made is amazing."

When the lunch was finished, Alina and Sally cleared the table and stacked the dishwasher while Ronnie made coffee. They went through to the sitting room to relax and talk over the latest developments in the search for clues about the old woman.

"So tell me what has been happing with you guys?" Sally asked.

"We decided to cast the Runes last Sunday and Ronnie helped me to cast a circle, nothing elaborate, just candles and incense."

"Really! Good for you Ronnie, I didn't realise that the mysteries interested you so much, I'm impressed. That would be a nice balance of male and female."

Alina went on to tell Sally about the three runes that they had chosen and the significance that they held.

"We were checking with the Rune book so that we didn't miss anything. It was Ronnie who noticed the illustration in the first one Eoh; it was a gypsy wagon.

I thought at first that it was referring to Ronnie because he was helping me, but I think the wagon was the connection because Ronnie went on to read the text in the book and it talked about a travelling family.

We could be just connecting dots influenced by the revelation that I have gypsy blood, but I don't think so."

"So the old woman may be from a travelling family Alina, what do you think Ronnie?"

"Yes I agree with that too, and something that hasn't been mentioned," he said cautiously "it may be someone from Alina's distant family."

Both girls exclaimed together, "Oh My God!"

"I didn't make that connection Ronnie."

"Nor did I," said Sally

They pondered on that for a few moments, each with their own thoughts then Ronnie continued.

"The next Rune had a rose in the illustration."

"You're joking, seriously, which one was it?"

Alina replied, "Thurizas, caution! I'm not sure if it is telling us to be cautious or if it was appearing because of the rose in my pouch."

"Oh I have no doubts about that Alina, I'm sure it's about the rose."

"Alina asked a third question to establish if we were looking for a person and where that person would be and she drew Lagu."

"Oh my God, in water, whoever it is may be nearby?"

"That's not all; the patio doors slammed open and when I went to close them the old woman was standing outside on the footpath. Ronnie saw her too."

Then Ronnie said, "Suddenly the room was filled with the scent of roses, and we may be way off base, but putting everything together we think we are looking for a girl, possibly the body of the old woman that appears to us, and we think she might be in the river. Her name might be Rosa."

Ronnie and Alina went on to tell Sally of their search at the Mitchell Library, and how Alina had dowsed over slips of paper to establish a year to search, and then did the same again searching by months.

"Alina had a hunch of the date that we would find something, but she wouldn't share. She put the date in her phone, and then, when we found an article that we thought could be relevant, she let me see the date and she was spot on."

"What did you find?"

"You have the copy of the piece don't you Ronnie."

"I put it in your workbox," he said and got up to fetch the paper that he had copied the text to and gave it to Sally.

Sally took it, studied it for a moment, and then began to read aloud, *'Police rushed to the area of Kinning Park to break up an unruly crowd of travellers who were causing a nuisance and creating fear and alarm by tramping through closes and banging on doors allegedly in search of a missing girl. No arrests were made and the unruly mob was disbanded.'*

'Oh my God! This is Kinning Park, but this new bit is now called the Waterfront, it must be here somewhere. That's quite upsetting; to think that a girl went missing is bad enough, but that perhaps she was never found…"

"Alina was upset too, but I think we have to put that behind us and try to find her if at all possible."

"How did you know the date Alina, I bet you used numerology didn't you? I knew you were good, but sometimes you really surprise me by how accurate you are. What's the next step?"

"I have been thinking about this for a few days, since we found the article really, I think I should go to the police."

"We'll come with you, what do you think Ronnie?"

Before Ronnie could answer, Alina said, "No, that's not a good idea. They will never believe us and will probably think we are time wasters. You have your reputation to think of Sally and you too Ronnie. I will go myself."

"What about your reputation?" they both asked simultaneously.

"Don't misunderstand me, please, I could never have done all this without your help, but I can't allow either of you to risk your livelihood on this."

Ronnie and Sally looked at each other. They both knew and understood Alina and although in some ways, she appeared vulnerable, and sometimes insecure, when she made up her mind about something there was no stopping her.

"Do Nancy and Davey know anything about this?" asked Sally.

"No, I haven't told them all the things that have been happening, they just know that the old woman appears in my dreams."

"Maybe you should talk it over with them," said Sally.

"Why?"

"If your parents were still here would you talk it over with them?"

Alina looked chastised. "Yes I guess I would."

"Well, Nancy and Davey have been like parents to you, and it's only my opinion, but I think you should tell them everything, and Aunt Nessie too, because when and if news of this breaks they will all be involved one way or another."

Alina had tears in her eyes.

"I don't want anyone's life to be disturbed by this, but I feel driven to follow this course. You are right, I know you are."

Ronnie reached over and held Alina's hand. "You do what you have to do Alina and we will be there for you no matter what the consequences are."

Ronnie and Sally hugged Alina comforting her.

"Ok I'll give Nancy and Davey a call and ask if they would like to come for dinner tonight. Do you want to nip across the hall and ask Auntie Nessie, Ronnie?"

Chapter 42

Alina, Sally and Ronnie shared in the making of spaghetti bolognaise; Ronnie chopped onions, garlic, and skinned tomatoes, Sally gathered and chopped oregano and parsley from the herb pots that Alina had started growing on her veranda, while Alina browned the minced beef. Sally went on to preparing garlic bread and then when everything was in the bolognaise pot Alina added tomato puree, grated parmesan and a stick of celery.

"Celery?" said Sally.

"Shh, secret ingredient," laughed Alina and left the pot to simmer. The table was set for six and Ronnie had gone to the off license to pick up a couple of bottles of red wine.

There was almost an air of apprehension as they sat in the sitting room waiting for everyone to arrive. Alina was nervous, but no one was surprised about that, as what she was about to tell Nancy, Davey, and Auntie Nessie, might come as a bit of a shock to them.

Auntie Nessie was watching from her window for Nancy and Davey's car to arrive so that she could go into Alina's at the same time. She gave it the right amount of time and opened her front door, which was opposite Alina's, and they all went in together.

Auntie Nessie was wearing a plain grey skirt with a twin set in her favourite colour of pale pink that suited her grey hair and smooth complexion. She had added a hint of blusher, pink lipstick and had on a matching set of pearl earrings and necklace. She had already met Nancy and Davey a couple of times and they enjoyed catching up and asking after each other.

Nancy was wearing a fine knit dress in bottle green and although her hair was grey now she often used a mid brown rinse. The effect as the rinse washed out and as Nancy's hair grew, gave her bands of silver at each side and tonight she had gathered her hair up from the sides with two attractive slide combs. Davey as a courtesy to the fact that he was out for dinner had changed out of his baggy grey trousers and favourite holey cardigan and T shirt at Nancy's insistence, and was wearing smart jeans and a white polo shirt.

Ronnie entertained the three of them and offered something to drink while Alina and Sally went to the kitchen to put on the spaghetti, warm the garlic bread, and prepare a side salad. The water had been on the boil so there wasn't long to wait before everyone sat at the table with delicious food in front of them.

Sally, Alina, and Ronnie had talked about how and when they should tell the family; and they decided rather than tell all of it before or after dinner, they would try to keep it casual, as casual as it could be anyway, and tell them during dinner. This wasn't going to be an easy task as Nancy, Davey, and Nessie were so busy chatting and laughing, taking turns at exchanging snippets while they ate, that no one could get a word in edgeways.

Sally, Alina, and Ronnie looked at each other grinning and making eyes at their elders. Ronnie held his fork in his hand level with his wine glass, he mouthed and nodded to Alina "Will I?", and he motioned ringing his fork against the glass to attract them.

Alina and Sally both laughed, Alina nodded and Ronnie tinkled his fork against his glass and made a coughing sound "Ahu mmm."

They looked up as one, and everyone laughed together and settled down as they wondered if there was going to be an announcement. Nessie and Nancy gave a quick glance and a secret knowing look to each other, thinking that the announcement was going to be one concerning rings and they were equally happy to think that.

There was an empty silence, and as they waited for news to fill it as Ronnie said encouragingly, "Alina has something to tell everyone, go on Alina."

"Recently memories of little things have been coming to me and there is a reason for that, I'm sure now. I suppose I should start with a fairy story that my mother told me when I was a little girl. Until a few months ago I had forgotten the story, but now I remember all of it."

She told this story...

"Once upon a time, long, long, ago there was a group of gypsies who travelled in tall colourful wagons. Big wheels held the wagons up and long wooden poles attached the horses that pulled them along from place to place. The wooden insides and outsides of the wagons were painted in bright colours with hints of gold here and there.

The big group had smaller groups, and each of the smaller groups had their own place that they returned to when they were not travelling from fair to fair, or farm to farm, but they travelled often and getting back to their own place was like a holiday. There were hundreds of people in the big group, they were all there together;

And then my mother would sing this song"

Alina sang it just as her mother would have.

"The Morrisons', Cunninghams', and the Stewarts', too

The Boswells' and Marshalls', the Deadmans', sure.

Douglas, and Wilson, Donnelly and Kelly

There they all were under the trees.

Not forgetting the family of Lees.

Some families would go this way and some families would go that, but always, always, always, they would come back to that place that was theirs; they called it home.

In every group, every woman was every child's granny, or mother, or auntie, or cousin or sister. In every group, every man was every child's Grandpa, Father, uncle, cousin, or brother. They called it family.

You see, to travelling folk, family is everything. Family is all you need. When you have family, you feel safe and loved, but when you don't have family, you always search and wonder.

In one particular family there were two daughters who were princesses, and both princesses were beautiful, good, clean, and kind.

The little princess loved her older sister and learned how to wash the pots and clear the fire before the wagons moved in the mornings. They travelled all around Scotland, but the princesses liked Ayrshire the best. The older princess she liked it best when they went to Dalgarven Mill in Kilwinning. The miller was a nice man and gave them fresh baked bread and bags of flour in exchange for his horses being shod.

The miller had a son who was about the same age as the older princess and they knew each other from when they were little. They waved eagerly when they saw each other, and if there were a moment or two to chat or play, they would take advantage of it, but as they grew, so did their friendship for each other. Soon they were no longer just friends; they loved each other; they would steal a moment to run in the fields with the sun in their hair and smiles on their young faces.

The princess sang a song when they were together, and the miller's son would say to her, 'Sing me your song Gypsy Girl' and she would sing in her lilting voice."

Alina sang,

"Meet me tonight by the campfire

Come with me over the hill.

Let us be married tomorrow

Please let me whisper 'I will'

What if the neighbours are talking?

Who cares if your friends stop and stare?...

One day the song became true when the miller's son asked the princess to marry him.

'I can't, I can't! She cried.'

'Don't you love me?' he asked.

'With all my heart, but you and me are different and I can only marry from my kind.'

Her heart broke as she realised her family and her group would never agree to the union.

'Run away with me,' he said.

On the night that she ran away, the older princess told the little princess that she was leaving.

"But we're family?" little sister cried.

"I know and I will always love you, but little sister, when you find love that pure and true it does not matter if you are different kinds, if you find love don't let it go."

And with that the older sister slipped out into the night and was gone, but for a long, long, time she missed her family, and she would sing her song,

'Meet me tonight by the campfire

Come with me over the hill.

Let us be married tomorrow

Please let me whisper 'I will'

What if the neighbours are talking?

Who cares if your friends stop and stare..."

There was total silence in the room when Alina finished talking.

Alina continued with her thoughts and feelings.

"I didn't notice until Mum and Dad died, but I think there has always been a feeling of not knowing who I am. It came to a head when they died and more so after I left JJ. At first, I just thought it was the transition, but it all makes sense now and I want to know who I am and where I come from. What makes me who I am? Why do I yearn for family? I think the old woman must be family, I want to find her, to see how I can help her, and I think I know where she is."

Alina excused herself and went to the bathroom to wash her face. Her insides were in turmoil and in her mind, all she could see were the silent looks of concern on the faces of Nancy, Davey, and Nessie.

Chapter 43

For a few moments after Alina had left the room everyone was lost in their own thoughts. Alina had touched their hearts with her words, and then Nancy broke the silence when she turned to Davey and said,

"Poor lass, I never knew she felt like that Davey."

"Nor I, and it saddens me to think that we missed it. She always just gets on with things."

"And all this time she has been hurting inside, Nessie said, and thinking of us before herself,"

Ronnie and Sally began to tell them more about the dreams and the appearances when Alina came back through to the dining room. The conversation continued as Ronnie, Alina, and Sally talked about the various methods that they had used to find information, summing up with the newspaper clipping.

"The thing is," said Davey, "the newspaper clipping says a young girl went missing, but it's an old woman who appears to you. I don't understand that; wouldn't it be the young girl who would appear to you?"

"I don't know either Davey, but it doesn't alter the fact that the woman keeps appearing and it seems to be connected to the young girl. I just know that I have to go to the police and ask them to search in the Clyde. I am sure they will think I am some kind of fool, and I am worried that the newspapers get a hold of this and that's why I wanted to forewarn you. I don't want you to be troubled by this."

Davey stood up and went around to Alina on the other side of the dining table, "Come here lass." He took her hand and she stood up as he wrapped his arms around her. "We may not be your real family, but we love you very much and we will support you no matter what you decide to do."

"Hear, hear," chanted Nancy and Nessie. And everyone gathered around Alina offering their unconditional support.

"Let's go through to the sitting room and I'll pour us all a drink," Ronnie said.

"Not for me thanks, I'm driving."

"Stay the night, Nancy, Davey; you can use my spare room since Sally has Alina's."

Nancy and Davey looked at each other and nodded.

"That's kind of you Nessie I think we will be happy to take you up on your offer." Then to Ronnie he said, "A whisky or a brandy would be great."

Ronnie poured drinks for everyone while the women cleared the table and stacked the dishwasher. The task done, they joined the men in the sitting room.

"So what's the next step Alina?" Davey asked.

"I will go to the police station at Helen Street on Monday, I want to think about what I am going to say over the weekend, and I think I will go out with my dowser tomorrow and walk a few hundred yards around here."

They discussed the recent events over drinks and then Nancy and Davey went next door with Nessie. Sally was leaving to have a couple of days at home in Largs the next morning, so she kissed Ronnie and Alina good night before going to the spare room. Ronnie and Alina relaxed on the sofa and talked about how the news had gone down with their families.

"They just took it in their stride," Alina said.

"Did you expect them to react in a different way?"

"Well I didn't really know what to expect."

"They love you very much Alina and Aunt Nessie already loves you too, so it's understandable that they would want to support you, and I love you too. Come on, it's been a long day and you look worn out, let's go to bed."

The next day after breakfast, Nancy and Davey popped in to say bye to Alina and Ronnie before they left for home.

"Do you want to do anything over the weekend Alina?"

"I think I just want to lie about watching old westerns and be a couch potato; is there something that you want to do?"

He laughed, "Yes be a couch potato, watch old westerns with you, and we could be really lazy and order in later."

"Fantastic."

They took the time to themselves relaxing and trying to avoid the subject of dowsing for a body and seeing the police. Ronnie lounged back on the big sofa and Alina lay on the other end with her feet in Ronnie's lap. When they checked the TV planner, they saw that there was a John Wayne film, 'The Quiet Man', not exactly a western, but definitely worth watching. As they watched the old movie, Ronnie massaged Alina's feet and stroked her legs, such a little thing, but a tenderness that she had never experienced with JJ. She wasn't comparing JJ and Ronnie, but she was comparing the way Ronnie treated her. He treated her with consideration, kindness, and tenderness and when he loved her, he treated her as though she was his Goddess.

He turned, his gaze distracted from the film,

"What?"

"Nothing."

He was grinning at her, "I could feel you staring."

"I was just thinking."

"About what?"

"About you and the way you care, just the things that you do. You make me feel happy inside."

"Alina, I will do everything I can to make you happy and that's a promise; come here."

She swung round on the sofa as he pulled her onto his lap and wrapped his arms around her.

Ronnie made sure that Alina had a restful weekend. He knew the strain that she had been under and he knew that worse was to come on Monday. He wanted to go to the police with her, but he also knew that she had ideas about her independence and that, at this stage in their relationship, she would consider his insistence controlling rather than supportive as intended. He would be close by so that he would be there for her when she would need him most.

Chapter 44

There was quietness between Ronnie and Alina on Monday morning as they showered, dressed, and had breakfast. Alina was nervous, and Ronnie was concerned for her and the reaction that she might get when she went to the police station.

"I have been thinking about this and I have decided that I want to ask a professional dive company for information first, before I go to the police."

"That's probably a really good idea Alina."

"Do you know anyone?"

"No, but I'll Google it."

They went through to the office together and their search revealed several dive companies, however, Clyde Commercial Diving had a local telephone number, and being quite close to where they were it seemed the ideal place to start. The director's name was Jim Patterson. Alina made the call and asked to speak to him, but he was out of the office.

The receptionist said that he was returning from the highlands having been involved in the repair of a Cal Mac ferry, but she took Alina's number and said that she would pass a message to him and he would call her back. An hour later Jim Patterson called, and arranged to meet her the next day at ten am at his office in Loanbank Quadrant, just off Helen Street.

Alina breathed a sigh of relief after the call, not because she was relieved that he had called back, but because she had another day before it would begin.

"Come on Alina, let's go to a property auction."

"What? Are you buying property?"

"Not necessarily, but we should do something completely different today and there is a property auction in Kilmarnock Road."

Alina's mood brightened immediately.

"I've never been to a property auction."

"It's exciting, I'm sure you'll enjoy it and it will be a distraction."

They went in Ronnie's BMW; the Waterfront was a convenient location to access anywhere in Glasgow since it was so close to the access points for all major and minor routes. Ronnie drove his BMW out of the waterfront, turned left towards the junction at Morrison Street, and then they followed the turns to pick up the M77, which led them directly to Kilmarnock Road, only ten minutes from the apartment.

There was an air of anticipation and excitement in the auction hall as people shuffled about whispering to each other, trying to look as though they weren't interested, and waiting for that moment when they would start bidding for the property that they wanted. Some people were there to buy homes for themselves, but many of the buyers were property developers.

Alina found it fascinating to watch, and from time to time Ronnie would draw her attention to someone or other so that she could watch how he or she bid. It was a fascinating process and it served Ronnie's purpose of distracting Alina from her concerns.

After the auction they went for a bar meal at one of the local pubs and then headed back to the apartment. They called in to see Aunt Nessie and took Jock for a walk before spending the evening with Nessie in her apartment.

Alina asked Ronnie to stay the night when they left Nessie's apartment.

"I would like you to go with me to meet Jim Patterson tomorrow."

"Of course I will."

"But I still want to go to the police station myself."

"I understand Alina, stop worrying, we will take things one step at a time and I am going to be here whenever you need me."

The next day they went to meet Jim Patterson at Clyde Commercial Diving as arranged. Jim was actively involved with Strathclyde Police Underwater Search Unit, and his experience included diver training, and operations including recovery of missing persons or articles.

They found that Jim was very helpful in answering Alina's questions, and he explained some of the historical facts about the Underwater Search Unit set up in the 1960's after the Peter Manuel murders. Alina asked about the possibility of finding a body and the condition a body would be in had it been in the Clyde for almost a hundred years, and Jim explained about the previous dredging of the Clyde by the Clyde Navigation Trust, which became the Clyde Port Authority. Jim told her that if a body was there it was likely to be below six feet of silt unless it had been disturbed for some reason, and the likelihood was that only bones would remain.

Jim told her that her first point of contact would be the police and that she should contact them in the first instance, and that they would do a search. He went on to explain that the resources that the police had these days may restrict the amount of time they could search, but assured them that if they were unhappy he would be willing to search on their behalf.

Alina asked Jim how much notice Clyde Port Authority required, thinking that it could take weeks for consent, but Jim explained that it was a safety notification to the CPA so that shipping in the area would know that the divers were in the water. He shook their hands as they left and assured them that he would do what he could if it became necessary, and both Ronnie and Alina thanked him for his input and advice.

"He was so helpful wasn't he Ronnie, and he didn't seem to be put off by the fact that I am a psychic or that we were trying to trace a body that we really didn't know for sure was there."

"Do you feel more confident now?"

"Yes I do; would you take me to the new police station now?"

Ronnie drove his car out of the car park and turned right into Helen Street. It only took them five minutes to get there, and Ronnie dropped Alina off at the main door while he went to wait in the visitor's car park.

Her heart was thumping as she went through the blue swing doors and into the reception area. Several officers were going about their business moving between offices and there were some rough looking individuals sitting in waiting areas.

For two pins, Alina would have turned and run out of the station, but she willed herself to the reception desk and stood in front of it facing a uniformed police officer.

"Miss?"

"Can I speak to someone in the Underwater Search Unit please?"

The officer looked at her as though she had horns.

"Can you tell me what your business with them is and I'll see what I can do?"

"I would really rather just speak to one of them direct thank you."

"There might not be anyone here that can help you, so if you tell me why you need to speak with them I will try to help you."

"Is there somewhere that I can explain privately?"

Alina could see that he was exasperated, but she stood her ground and looked him in the eye.

"Give me a minute?"

He left the desk and a few moments later a door in the reception area opened and the officer called her over and asked her to take a seat.

"Someone will be with you in a minute."

She assumed that he went back to his desk duty so she waited where she was, but began to wonder if she was being ignored because it was about fifteen or twenty minutes before anyone came to see her. A young constable came through the door.

"Can I help you miss?"

"I wanted to see someone from the Underwater Search Unit."

"There is no one here from that unit so if you tell me what it's about I will try to help."

"I wondered if they could do a search for a body in the Clyde."

He raised his eyebrows and drew back at the nature of her request.

"Where is this body?"

"Near the Waterfront development where I live."

His attitude changed and became more professional.

"Let me take some details."

He opened a document on the computer on the desk in front of her and asked her for her name address and occupation. She felt uncomfortable saying professional psychic, as she knew what misconceptions this would lead to, and the minute she gave her occupation his eyebrows rose again, but he made no comment.

"Now tell me about this body, where did you see it?"

"Well that's the problem, you see I haven't actually seen it, but I know it's there."

"Did you overhear someone talking about the body?"

"No, you see, the thing is, I have been having dreams, and all this goes back to the 1920's..."

Before she could say anymore, the constable put his hand up in front of her and stood up.

"Just give me a minute."

He went out of the door that he had come through and she heard him saying, "Is this a windup?"

Then there was muted conversation and she could only hear a few words, dead body, psychic, time waster, and then a lot of laughter. She felt humiliated, a lump formed in her throat, her lips began to tremble, and tears began to run down her face. She stood up and without further ado, she left the office that she was in and hurried past the reception and out of the police station to look for Ronnie who was already watching for her coming out. He drove the car forward meeting her at the entrance to the station. He knew by the tears that it had not been a good experience.

Chapter 45

On the short journey home Alina was quietly sobbing to herself, more from embarrassment and frustration that anything else, and Ronnie let her cry believing that it was better for her than holding it in. When she stopped crying she wiped her eyes and blew her nose trying to compose herself.

"They laughed at me, they made me feel stupid and embarrassed."

She told him everything that had happened and asked him to take her back to Jim Patterson's office.

"Alina I think you have been through enough, why don't you give me his number and I will call him and ask him to organise a search?"

Alina took her phone from her handbag and handed it to Ronnie. He pulled over to the side of the road and made the call.

"Hi there Jim its Ronnie here, I came in earlier with Alina, we would like you to go ahead with a search please."

"I take it that it didn't go well at the police station then?" he asked.

"No; quite the opposite, so we would like to go ahead with the search please."

"Well you followed proper procedure and you can't be faulted for that. I have a space in the diary tomorrow morning around ten o'clock if that's good for you?"

Ronnie agreed to the appointment and gave Jim Alina's address.

"I'm taking you home now and no arguments; you cannot carry this burden on your own. You need a big brandy and some rest."

Alina hadn't the energy to argue so she just lay back in the comfort of the big saloon car and closed her eyes.

When they arrived home, Ronnie ran her a bath, put candles on each corner of the bathtub, and sprinkled some Himalayan Bath Salts and some bubble bath into the water. He went through to the sitting room and pressed play on the stereo. He knew that chances were whatever was first to play would be ambient and it was.

Alina was sitting on the sofa with her eyes closed going over in her mind the frustration and embarrassment that she was feeling. She opened her eyes when Ronnie took her hand and led her into the bathroom.

"Oh Ronnie, that's just so lovely, thank you."

"Get your clothes off and get into the bath and I'll bring you a brandy."

She did as she he told her without another thought. As she sank into the warm water, she felt all her cares leaving her, at least for a while. She lay back in the water and sipped at the brandy; she could feel the warmth of it easing the anguish she felt inside as the water eased the tension in her muscles. She emptied her mind and rested.

The next morning, refreshed after a sound dreamless sleep, Alina was ready when Jim arrived. Ronnie opened the door for him and he gave Jim a brief outline of the events that brought them to where they were. Jim took it all in his stride; clearly, he was a sensitive open-minded man who understood that he was playing an important role in this drama.

Alina and Ronnie went outside with Jim and Alina began to use her dowser. She held it as before in her right hand with the chain suspended over her index finger while her thumb held it in place. She walked from the edge of her entrance to the left towards the Glasgow Quay. She had only gone about ten yards when the dowser began to spin furiously. Ronnie and Jim looked at each other for a moment and then Jim picked up his mobile and began to make a call to his office.

"Christine, prepare a risk assessment, other paperwork and notify Clyde Port Authority of a dive tomorrow morning from ten a.m., and then check with some of the other divers and see who will be available to partner me on the dive. I'll text you the coordinates and expected duration shortly."

Jim took a permanent marker from his pocket and made a mark on the paving where the dowser had indicated and then they went back to the Alina's apartment. There were contracts to be completed and Alina made Jim some coffee while he was preparing them. Once they were completed and signed, they shook hands and Jim left, promising to be back at ten the following morning.

The next morning around nine thirty, two vans arrived and parked near the area that Jim had marked. The two men with Jim began to unload their gear, various tools and prepared their equipment for the dive.

"Do you want to go down and watch Alina?"

"I don't know, I'm not sure, it will be terrible if they find something and terrible if they don't. Yes, I want to be there."

Together they went down to watch. A small crowd began to gather, curious about the goings on. This was Alina's worst fear, knowing that anyone in the crowd could call the newspapers and she didn't want that to happen.

Each diver took turns in the deep murky water, which was so dark that it was impossible to see your hand in front of your face. Powerful flashlights did little to make things any easier for them. Turn after turn they took until about two o'clock in the afternoon Jim, who was currently diving, surfaced, and gave a thumbs up. Alina assumed that they must be giving up for the day at least, as Jim was helped out of the water. He took off his facemask, tanks, and flippers, and barefoot walked over to Alina. He looked at Ronnie, then back at Alina, and said, "Found a human bone."

That was the last thing Alina heard until she came to sitting on the walkway, as she had simply passed out, and both Ronnie and Jim had caught her and lowered her gently to the ground.

"Give me a minute, I have to call the Strathclyde Police Underwater Search Unit. They have to secure the scene until we recover the remains."

The other divers were already pushing people back and creating a barrier around the area.

Ronnie took Alina home and called Nessie to come over. Ronnie was already making Alina drink hot sweet tea when Nessie arrived.

"Sit with her Auntie Nessie I've got to go back down."

Within minutes, the place was swarming with police who were erecting barricades and screens to isolate the scene. The Underwater Search Unit arrived and spoke at length with Jim and then they too began to dive. An officer from the Underwater Search Unit came to the apartment with Ronnie to interview Alina, to ask her how she knew about the body and why she hadn't informed the proper authority.

Alina did her best to explain what had led her to believe that a body was there, and explained that she had been to the police, but they had laughed at her. The officer did not have much to say about Alina's treatment, but he didn't look very pleased.

"It may take some time to recover all the remains, but we will keep you informed," he said before he left. The CID arrived next and began to question, Alina treating her almost as though she had done something wrong, until Auntie Nessie stood up and gave them a piece of her mind. They too left saying that they would be back.

Ronnie sent Sally a quick text.

"We hired divers Remains found in Clyde. When are you free?"

Within minutes, a text arrived from Sally.

"Cancelling my appointments. I will be there first thing in the morning."

Then the telephone started to ring and Nessie answered,

"This is Mrs Brodie; can I take a message for Alina?"

She didn't hear the name of the person calling, but she did hear the word 'newspaper' and promptly put the phone down.

With some considerable coaxing Nessie managed to steer Alina into the bedroom and into bed.

"A good sleep is what you need now. This has all been a bit of a shock for you. I'll stay here, don't you worry about a thing."

Alina was asleep within minutes and thankfully didn't hear the telephone continuing to ring.

"We should unplug that land line Ronnie."

He did just that and then began to pace.

"This is so hard on Alina, I think I will give Nancy and Davey a call," he said, and used his mobile phone.

"Hello?"

"Davey it's started, divers found human remains and the place is swarming with police and newspapers."

"Oh lord, how is Alina taking all this?"

"Nessie has put her to bed and for the moment she is fast asleep, but it was a shock for her. I suppose part of her didn't want to believe that there was a body."

"Nancy and I will be over shortly."

"Why don't you wait till the evening; it may be a bit calmer then?"

"Perhaps you're right, I'll speak with Nancy when she comes back from the shops, see what she thinks."

"I'll call you when Alina wakes up."

Just as he closed the phone, the external door went. He pressed the buzzer to see who was there.

"It's Jim Patterson."

"Come on up Jim, but don't let any reporters try to sneak in."

Ronnie opened the door to let Jim in and shook his hand as he entered the apartment.

"That's us finished now Ronnie, I must admit I don't really know what to say. I was open to the possibility that we might find something, but you know her accuracy with that dowser was astounding. I was speaking to the inspector downstairs at the scene and gave him a little of the background. We both agree she could probably help a lot of people."

"She is sound asleep just now; she will glad that you called and you are probably right, but she is in no fit state to help anyone just now, she needs time to reconcile all this and we still don't know who we have found."

"Well anyway, tell her I called and I would be happy to work with her anytime."

"She'll appreciate that Jim. Can I get you a coffee or something?"

"No, we're packing up and heading back to the office, just give her my regards and tell her to pop in and see me anytime."

Later that night Nancy, Davey, and Sally arrived and Alina had already showered and changed. Nessie had watched over her like a guard dog throughout the day; when she was sure that Alina was all right, she roasted a chicken and cooked a big pot of chicken soup to feed everyone.

Chapter 46

The Underwater Search Unit took several days to recover all the remains and take them to the city morgue for the pathologist to attempt to discern the cause of death, and establish whether a crime had been committed. Newspapers carried various headlines: -

'Human Bones Found in Clyde.'

'Glasgow Psychic Finds Body.'

There was even a mention on the television, but through it all, Alina and the rest of the family refused to be named or interviewed, and neighbours who may have known them kept tight-lipped. Some Glasgow residents came along to the spot that the bones were recovered from and laid flowers at the scene.

A few weeks later, a police inspector came to the apartment; Ronnie had been staying there permanently since the discovery so he pressed the buzzer to release the external door and was waiting to let him in.

"I've just come to let you know that the tests have been completed, and it has been established that the remains were that of a young girl, probably between fifteen and eighteen years old, and that she was murdered. The pathologist believes that the remains have been in the Clyde for around a hundred years."

Ronnie and Alina looked at each other.

"When will the body be released?" asked Alina.

"There are still some formalities to go through, but probably within the next week. I will let you know for sure. I take it you want to claim responsibility for the burial of the remains?"

"Yes, thank you."

"I wonder if I might speak to you on another matter."

"Of course."

"The thing is, we have open unsolved cases of missing persons and I wondered if you would be interested, you and your team, in having a look at them?"

Again, Ronnie and Alina looked at each other. Alina laughed for a moment, "Are you serious? I don't have a team, this has been an experience that we all shared, but we're not a team."

"Perhaps it's something that you would consider; these are my contact details and the numbers listed will take you directly to me, I hope you will think about this as I am sure that you will be able to help us close some cases and put some people's minds to rest."

He stood up and handed Alina his card.

"I won't take up any more of your time; I'll let you know when the remains are ready for collection."

"I'm sorry, forgive me, I didn't mean to sound flippant, you just took me by surprise."

"No offence taken, just get in touch when you have had time to consider my offer and we will talk about the possibilities some more."

After the inspector left, Ronnie said, "I wonder what Sally will make of that offer?"

"I do too, we can ask her, she will be here tomorrow. She sent a text, said she had news. She said not to make any plans."

The next day Sally arrived; she was always excited and upbeat, but there was something about her enthusiasm this time that was different. She could hardly wait to take her jacket off and settle down.

"Sit down, both of you. I want to tell you what happened yesterday. I was in Carlisle and a client came across to me for a reading. I told her to sit down and waited while she got comfortable, and then when I asked for her name and address as per usual, she said, 'Joanne Miller'. I nearly fell off my chair, but I kept it together and began to prepare the cards.

I kept looking at her and I could see that she was a bit uncomfortable to the point where she actually asked me if something was wrong. Anyway, I told her to put her hands over the cards and think of her questions, and then as always I fanned them out and told her to choose the ones that she wanted me to read. She made her selection and I began to place them in the horoscope spread. Alina I saw America! I had to stop reading for her, I knew it was your Joanne, so I just told her everything, and it is her!"

"No Way!"

Alina jumped out of her seat as Sally did the same. Ronnie watched in amazement as the two of them, holding hands, danced on the spot.

"Can you believe it! She came right up to my table. She is so excited."

"I can't wait to talk to her."

"You won't have to; she will be here in about an hour."

Alina was pacing now. She had never felt this excited about anything.

"She's coming here? In an hour?"

"Actually they're coming here, her husband John and their daughter Rosemarie were waiting in the lounge of the hotel, so she went to fetch them and they know everything. The three of them are coming, your family Alina, your family."

Sally started to cry and Alina joined her. The two girls hugged each other and quietly sobbed with the emotion of this new development. Ronnie could only stand by and shake his head, but deep down he felt the power of the emotion as it flooded through him.

"What the hell," he thought to himself and wrapped his arms around both of them.

Alina could hardly contain her excitement, she kept going back and forward to look out of the window.

"Oh my God! I think this is them," she said, as a large white Bentley drove slowly into the Waterfront.

"I have to go down," she said as she rushed to the door.

Alina reached the main door as they pulled in to park. The registration plate read 1986 JM. It had to be them. The woman in the passenger seat caught sight of Alina and waved and the man looked over and grinned.

Joanne got out of the car, ran towards Alina, and threw her arms around her.

"You have the look of family about you," she said, and kissed her. Alina felt as though she was looking at a younger version of her mother, but with dark hair. She was every bit as fashion conscious as her mother too, and she looked smart in a beautiful black knitted dress with diagonal white stripes and chunky jewellery.

"I might be your cousin, or even your aunt several times removed, but who cares, you're family. Meet John and Rosemarie."

John was a bear of a man, dark haired, tall and broad shouldered. He looked as strong as an ox. When he hugged Alina, he hugged her so tight she could hardly breathe. He was in casual wrangler jeans, tan cowboy boots, a white polo shirt and a Giorgio Armani belt, which was a nice salute to style, and then there was young Rosemarie.

Alina felt as though she was meeting a young niece, and she was so pretty. Long brown hair cascaded down her back and blue eyes looked at her coyly as she came towards Alina for an embrace. Her jeans had sparkle down each side seam and the matching denim jacket had more diamante on the shoulders. They all had tears in their eyes as Alina took them inside and upstairs to the apartment.

Ronnie had called Nancy and Davey, they were on their way over, and Nessie was already there. Everyone was talking at the same time and the air of excitement was palpable. Young Rosemarie was watching in almost bewildered amusement and tolerance of her elders then Nancy and Davey arrived, and it all started again.

Chapter 47

When they had all finally settled down, Joanne began to give Alina some information that would make things clear for her regarding her dreams and the appearance of the old woman.

"Our direct lineage goes back to Coralina Kelly who ran away to marry Robert Miller. I know from Sally that you are familiar with this side of the story, but there is more. We travellers are very committed to family and we like to keep ourselves to ourselves. In those days, it was very rare for a gypsy girl to marry a gorger, someone that wasn't a gypsy, and gorgers frowned on any of their kind marrying gypsies.

When Coralina and Robert ran away it broke two families' hearts, and caused a lot of trouble at the time. Soon it was too late to find them and no one who knew would admit to knowing where they were. They went on to have the family that you know of, but later we all began to share stories, and as we know, it Coralina had a sister called Mary.

Mary married John and they had only one child, which was unusual as in those days' big families were common. Rosa their daughter grew up and married Edward. They say he was a fantastic carpenter and that he had carved a little wooden rose when he was only a boy, and he gave it to Rosa when she was about ten or twelve."

Alina by this time had paled, and she was staring open mouthed at Joanne. She looked at Sally, and Sally said, dragging out the syllables, "I knooow!"

Joanne picked up the story again.

"From time to time, Coralina was able to get messages to Mary, but as a child Coralina made Mary swear to keep her secret, and she was afraid to tell anyone that Coralina kept in touch so she shared her secret with no one. Coralina heard about Mary and John's wedding and Rosa's birth, and later all about Rosa and Eddie's wedding on the Tinkers Heart.

Sadly, Rosa died of pre-eclampsia as she was giving birth to her daughter Rosie. There are a lot more stories to tell, but we know that when Rosie was about sixteen she went missing while she was out selling from her basket. The story handed down is that while Eddie was searching he found the wooden rose that he had carved for Rosa at the corner of St James Street and Paisley Road West. St James Street has since been renamed Seaward Street."

"Oh my God! That's just down the road," said Alina, and Joanne nodded as she had already done some research herself. Joanne continued.

"Rosie had been carrying the carved rose for a few years so when Eddie found it he knew that she was around somewhere, but the police never found any sign of her. Sally told me your story and about the dreams that you were having. She told me about the old woman and the remains that have been recovered."

Joanne started to cry and Alina immediately went to kneel beside her chair to comfort her.

"You have been seeing old Mary, Coralina's sister, and the remains that were found are young Rosie."

Everyone in the room had tears in their eyes or was openly weeping; finding someone's remains was one thing, finding out later that those remains belonged to your family was something else entirely, and everyone in the room felt that pain.

"We are all so grateful to you Alina, and to Ronnie and Sally for the part that you played in this experience. The story told over the years is that hundreds searched for Rosie, and many never gave up hope of finding her. Those that remember will always be grateful.

We would like to be involved in the funeral arrangements. Janefield Cemetery is where the rest of the family are and if you have no objection, we would like that to be her final resting place, and please do not take any offence, but you will not have to pay for anything. Everyone will contribute to Rosie's burial."

Although for a short while the mood was subdued, it wasn't very long before things got back to normal. Joanne, John, and Rosemarie agreed to stay for a few days at Nessie's apartment as she had two spare rooms, and then they all went out to dinner at the Hilton in Glasgow.

They devoted the next few days to arranging with the city morgue for the release of Rosie's remains, and with the undertakers to set the date for the funeral. They agreed on the following week. Joanne, John, and Rosemarie were going home to Carlisle for a few days, but before they left, Joanne had something to tell Alina.

"Do you remember how Sally and I met?"

"Yes, you went to get your cards read."

"Yes that's right; John and I were undecided about whether we should stay in the UK and where we should stay, or whether we should return to the States. There have been so many opportunities, but we couldn't make up our minds. Anyway, I just wanted to tell you that we have taken this as a sign and we have made up our minds. We are going to stay and we will be looking at houses and business opportunities here, in Glasgow."

Alina threw her arms around Joanne.

"I'm so glad Joanne, it's going to be wonderful having you all here."

All too soon, the day of the funeral arrived. Joanne had arranged the transport and at ten a.m., a large black stretch limo arrived to pick up Alina, Ronnie, Sally, Nessie, Nancy, and Davey. Everyone was dressed in black as a sign of respect, and everyone wore a red rose on his or her clothing as a token to Rosie.

Joanne and her family followed behind in another black stretch limo, and as the cars turned out of the Waterfront estate, they caught sight of a beautiful white horse drawn carriage. Two police motorcycle riders escorted the two cars and the horse drawn hearse. Alina and the rest of the party looked on at the amazing white carriage with glass sides and gold trim along the edges.

Four white horses pulled the carriage, steered by two coachmen wearing formal black long coats and top hats. Inside the glass carriage was Rosie's white coffin, a wreath of red roses that spelled out 'Rosie McGuigan' resting against the side of it, and white rose petals were scattered all over the top and sides of the coffin.

The four white horses held their heads proudly as though they were aware of the importance of their task. White plumage decorated the tops of their heads and the bridles and harnesses were white leathers with highly polished brasses.

Alina was stunned to see police controlling the traffic and hundreds of cars all parking to attend the funeral. While the carriage waited, they got out of their car at the same time as Joanne and her family, and together they walked silently behind the carriage. As they walked hundreds of travellers joined the procession all without exception wearing a red rose.

Alina stood with Ronnie, Sally, Nancy, Davey, and Nessie to her right, and Joanne, John and Rosemarie to her left. The minister gave a beautiful talk on loss, hope, and never giving up, and then Alina watched as groups of mourners filed past and threw flowers and tokens as a sign of respect into Rosie's grave. As each family came past, they approached Alina shook her hand and offered her an envelope containing money and stated their family name: -

"The Boswells', for Rosie's headstone."

"The Wilsons', my family searched for a long time, this is for Rosie's headstone."

"The Morrisons', my granny told us Rosie's story, this is for her headstone."

And so it went on, so many names, so many emotions. Joanne had tears in her eyes, but she was smiling proudly. She whispered, "Family, you're one of us now."

Alina had no idea that she was sobbing, and Ronnie had tears streaming down his face. He was overwhelmed with love and pride for Alina.

The procession took an hour to complete and as the last mourner passed, Ronnie and Sally, followed by Joanne, John, and young Rosemarie, stepped forward to pay their last respects and drop their mementoes into the grave. Finally, Alina stepped forward and removed her pouch from around her neck. She opened it and took out the little wooden rose, then stood for a moment thinking of that day out with her mother when she was inexplicably drawn back into the antique shop to purchase it.

She thought of the journey that she had been on since, from seeing Mary in her dreams to finding Rosie. She felt Ronnie returning to her side and putting his arm around her waist, and then Joanne came and held her hand followed by John and Rosemarie. They all stood together united in their love and grief. Alina took a last look at the wooden rose, kissed it, and then threw it into Rosie's grave. Through her tears, she looked over the heads of the departing mourners, and there, in a sudden mist, was Mary younger, than in Alina's dreams. By her side was her Johnny in his First World War uniform. As the mist began to clear, she saw Rosa and Eddie hand in hand looking towards Rosie, running to towards her parents. Family united in love.

"Can you see that?" she whispered to Joanne.

"Family, Alina, we're always there for each other."

That's what it's all about, family, and that's the traveller's way.

The End

Coincidences:

The story began in my head with the image of a young woman gazing from her window, puzzling over the old woman who was staring up at her. Later, while chatting to my friend Rosie, she asked me what the book was going to be about, and when I began to tell her about the old woman Rosie suggested that she should be a gypsy. We laughed together as I said I would use her name and her daughter's name, Rosemarie, in the book.

Rosie phoned her sister Joanne, whom I had met once or twice, to tell her about the story that I was writing. Joanne, who is interested in genealogy, offered to help me with any research information, and of course, I had to name one of the characters Joanne. The details Joanne plied me with were invaluable.

A few days later, the story was taking shape and racing along and the first coincidence occurred. I break the news to my friend Rosie that the character Rosie disappears, never to be seen again.

"You're frightening me now," she says, "because that really happened."

"What happened?" I asked.

"In the 1920's a travelling girl from the Midlands disappeared and was never found again."

I had goose bumps and so did Rosie.

I continued to write, still racing through the story as though I was on a deadline. I reached part two of the story and had to think about a name for my heroine. People always say 'write about what you know' and I know Tarot, so my heroine had to be a psychic, and she had to have a name that would lend itself to that profession. I doodled, jotted down names, and even Googled, them to make sure that I wasn't using another psychic's name. Finally, I came up with Alina and thought no more about it.

Once I had put the bones of my story together, I went back to part one of the story to add character names and descriptions, and I began to email Joanne with research questions such as typical surnames, and where people would be married or buried. Joanne was a great help and promptly sent me the information that I was looking for. I began to develop my characters, and suddenly realised that Joanne had sent me Christian names and one of them was Coralina. I had named my Psychic Alina, which is found in Coralina! I must admit seeing that gave me a bit of a jolt and I wondered if I was channelling my story instead of creating it.

When I reached the part of the story where Alina begins to work with Runes, I knew in my mind exactly what Runes I would feature. On my bookshelf, I have several Rune books including one that I wrote. I turned and picked up the nearest to hand, just to check that I was using the right symbol. The book I picked is one I had used before I wrote my own version.

The last time I had looked at this book was when I was discussing with my husband Martin the illustrations that I wanted him to do for my Rune book, written in 2001. I opened the book at the Rune I wanted to use, and there, written in pencil was the word Gypsy Caravan. I had made this notation for my husband in 2001 as a brief hint at what I wanted him to use for the illustration. That astounded me and gave me goose bumps.

Later, I picked up the Rune book that I had written, and I was taken aback when I realised that one of the Runes that I planned to use had a rose in the illustration. So many coincidences, but it didn't stop there, one of my short stories in my book of Runes is about a travelling family!

Later in the story I realised that I would need logistical information concerning the recovery of a body from the Clyde, and Google came in handy again. I found the phone number for Clyde Commercial Diving and called to ask if anyone could help me. I was told that Jim Patterson was the director and I would need to speak to him, but he was in the Highlands inspecting a Cal Mac ferry that needed a repair. I laughed when I heard that, because the previous night I had been talking to my son Ian who is a purser on a Cal Mac ferry and he was part of the crew taking that same ferry in for the repair. Small world!

You will remember that in the beginning of the story Coralina runs away to marry a miller's son. In those days, it was common to have a surname that reflected your trade, so Coralina became Coralina Miller.

I told my friend Rosie that as a courtesy to her sister I was going to use her name, Joanne, as Alina's relative in the story. Rosie was delighted, and told me that Joanne would be thrilled. Much later in the book, when the character Joanne is located, I had to give her a surname, and I said to my hubby Martin that her surname would be Miller. "You can't use that," he said, "Coralina was a Miller."

"I know, but that was a hundred years ago, it has to be Miller, full circle." When it was done, I went to Rosie's house for coffee, my usual retreat, and told her the last part of the story, and about Joanne's appearance in the book. She jumped out of her chair.

"You're kidding me, you're kidding me. I must phone Joanne."

I thought she was excited because Joanne was included in the story, but Rosie knew that, so I was puzzled when she put the phone on loudspeaker. She told Joanne that I was there, and she asked Joanne to guess what surname I had used. Joanne was as mystified as I was and admitted that she didn't know.

"MILLER!" exclaimed Rosie. "She's called her Joanne Miller, and she has called her husband John."

It turns out that Joanne's surname is Miller and her husband's name is John. I should point out that I have only known Rosie for two years, and that I did not know Joanne's family name. So for me, the question remains; did I write this book, or did I somehow channel it?

Acknowledgements

I could never have written this story without the old woman that often appeared in my thoughts. I don't know who she was, but I am sure she had a hand in the creation of the wooden rose.

For the songs, I have to admit that I used artistic licence, because some of them did not exist until much later than the period that this book is set in.

The Tinkers Wedding was written by William Watt of Peeblesshire and first published in 1835.

The Yellow on the Broom was written by Adam McNaughton, a Glasgow songwriter and published in 1979.

John Duggan, who was a presenter on MID West Radio wrote the Road to Kildare.

Thanks also to Jim Patterson, the director of Clyde Commercial Diving who took time out of his busy schedule to explain the procedures concerning the recovery of remains in the Clyde.

With special thanks to the following people who helped to make this story and for their kind permission in allowing their names to be used.

Rosie, one of my closest friends, shared the experience and the frantic pace that the writing of this book took. Thanks also go to Rosie's sister Joanne, whose hobby is genealogy, plied me with relevant information that helped me to bring this story to life.

A special mention goes to my husband Martin who tolerated viewing the top of my head over my PC, helped with finding locations, created my timeline and family tree, which 1 found impossible to do, checked grammar and spelling without laughing at my dyslexic mistakes, and coped with my inability to focus on anything except 'the book'.

Before you go

I really hope that you do not find any errors in this book but if you do please forgive me. Dyslexia means that I often do not see what is right in front of my face and I have in the past, (more than once) uploaded the uncorrected manuscript.

I hope you enjoyed reading this story as much as I enjoyed writing it. Next in the series will be a prequel titled 'Before the Rose - the Gypsy's Curse' and the third in the series will be 'After the Rose' I hope you will follow the journey of The Rose Trilogy to its conclusion.

I would be so grateful if you could review my books on Amazon.

Blessings to you and yours, Soraya

*****

CPSIA information can be obtained
at www.ICGtesting.com
Printed in the USA
LVOW01s1807300916
506909LV00015B/714/P